Jake walked over and reached up a hand to Emma's face. He could see this was tearing her in two, breaking her heart.

He took a deep breath. Expelled it. Turned and paced the length of the bedroom. Looked at Emma. Looked out the window. Closed his eyes. Opened them and found her looking at him as though he might need medical attention. Which he might.

He paced some more, then stopped. "Marry *me*, Emma. We're both not looking for a real relationship or a real marriage. You'll save the farm."

What the hell? Had he just said that? Had he just proposed to Emma?

Good God, he had. Without thinking. *Gun to head, what are you going to do, Morrow?* Well, this was the answer.

A marriage proposal.

She stared at him. "Jake. You can't be serious. What could you possibly get out of this?"

"The best cook in Texas?" he said, managing a weak smile.

Had he just said *that*? What the hell was wrong with him? If anyone needed Emma's charm school for cowboys, he did. Good Lord.

* * *

HURLEY'S HOMESTYLE KITCHEN:
There's nothing more delicious than falling in love...

Dear Reader,

In my previous Special Edition, *The Cook's Secret ingredient*, the heroine's aunt Sarah takes the first step in reaching out to the twin sons she gave up for adoption as a teenager thirty-two years earlier. In *Charm School for Cowboys*, one of those twins, our handsome hero, Jake Morrow, has moved to Blue Gulch to connect with Sarah and begin the search for his biological twin brother, who was adopted by a different family.

But a few things hold Jake back from his quest. There's *a lot* going on at his Texas ranch. Like how his younger brother feels about Jake seeking his twin. Then there are his rough-around-the-edges ranch hands, who all have trouble in the romance department and sorely need charm school. Emma Hurley, the new cook at the Full Circle, is pregnant and on her own, yet tries to help the cowboys turn their luck around. Jake just might find himself unexpectedly transformed, too. Especially when Emma's father issues her an ultimatum and everyone discovers what family, in all its forms, really means...

I hope you enjoy Jake and Emma's story. I love to hear from readers! You can write me at authormegmaxwell@gmail.com or under my real name, melissasenate@yahoo.com. Meg Maxwell is a pen name, if you didn't already know!

Yours,

Meg Maxwell

Charm School
for Cowboys

———

Meg Maxwell

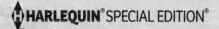
HARLEQUIN® SPECIAL EDITION®

Recycling programs
for this product may
not exist in your area.

ISBN-13: 978-0-373-62345-7

Charm School for Cowboys

Copyright © 2017 by Meg Maxwell

This edition published by arrangement with Harlequin Books S.A.

For questions and comments about the quality of this book,
please contact us at CustomerService@Harlequin.com.

Printed in U.S.A.

Meg Maxwell lives on the coast of Maine with her teenage son, their beagle and their black-and-white cat. When she's not writing, Meg is either reading, at the movies or thinking up new story ideas on her favorite little beach (even in winter) just minutes from her house. Interesting fact: Meg Maxwell is a pseudonym for author Melissa Senate, whose women's fiction titles have been published in over twenty-five countries.

Books by Meg Maxwell

Harlequin Special Edition

Hurley's Homestyle Kitchen

A Cowboy in the Kitchen
The Detective's 8 lb, 10 oz Surprise
The Cowboy's Big Family Tree
The Cook's Secret Ingredient

In dear memory of Greg Pope.

Chapter One

"I wouldn't date you if you were the last man in Texas, Hank Timber!"

Jake Morrow glanced up in time to see Fern, a neighboring rancher who'd dropped off the four billy goats he'd purchased for the Full Circle Ranch, scowling at his foreman. Fern stomped to her truck and sped off, dust and gravel flying in her wake.

Hank didn't even bother waving away the dirt and grit that now covered him. He shoved his hands in his pockets, his expression forlorn as Jake approached.

"Didn't go so well, huh?" Jake asked his foreman. Hank, twice divorced, had mentioned at breakfast this morning that he thought Fern was "darn pretty and had a way about her" and planned to ask her out to dinner at Hurley's Homestyle Kitchen, everyone's favorite restaurant in Blue Gulch.

Hank sighed. "I thought that rancher to rancher, I could ask her out by joking that we already had something in common—how we'd *both* stink of cow dung while chowing down on supper. Then I sniffed around her and nodded and laughed. Instead of saying yes to a date tonight, she got all mad." He shrugged, watching Fern's truck disappear down the Full Circle's long dirt drive.

Jake refrained from slamming his palm against his forehead. At this rate, Hank would be single forever. Of the four cowboys working for Jake at the Full Circle Ranch, his foreman wasn't even the most clueless when it came to women. No, Jake would say it was a four-way tie. Forty-two-year-old Hank had been in love with Fern since he laid eyes on her a month ago while listening to her presentation on calving season at the local rancher's association meeting. Twenty-five-year-old Golden, who'd earned the nickname from the motto about silence, was so shy and quiet he turned away any time the young woman he had a mad crush on, a Hurley's waitress, was around. Fifty-two-year-old Grizzle, who hadn't shaved or had a haircut in years, maybe a decade, spoke wistfully of his late wife and how he wished he could find someone as special, but had scared a little girl at the feed store in town with just the sight of him. Then there was Jake's own brother CJ, ten years his junior at twenty-two, who took full advantage of his good looks and ranch-honed muscles to play the field. CJ had left a trail of broken hearts and parents, older sisters, and bffs to storm up to Jake in town and let him know just what a "no-good lying player" his brother was. Charles John Morrow was a good guy, Jake knew that more than he knew just about anything, but when it came to love and romance, CJ was an absolute hot mess, a train wreck, as his neighbor's teenage daughter would put it. CJ would just say, *Well, what was I supposed to do? Propose? She just wasn't the one.* The Morrow brothers had been in Blue Gulch all of one month, and at least ten young women hadn't been "the one."

Jake couldn't relate to all this hankering for "the one." He'd been able to once, though. Five years ago he'd even gotten down on one knee and proposed with a skywriter spelling out the words in puffy white across the dusky sky. But his girlfriend Samantha wouldn't say yes without certain conditions being met, difficult conditions that Jake had realized she was probably right about and so had tried to meet. Jake was adopted and had no knowledge of his medical history. Samantha didn't feel comfortable starting a future, which would include children and a lifetime together, without knowing what was *in* that history. And so Jake, not quite comfortable with digging into a past he wasn't all that interested in, had gone through his late parents' documents, looking for information on the adoption agency that had handled his case so he could contact them.

What he'd found among those papers had shocked him.

Jake had a biological twin brother who'd been adopted by another family. The scrawled notation on a document didn't say anything else.

A twin brother—out there in this world.

Jake had lain awake night after night, thinking about the twin, wondering if they were identical or fraternal. If they were similar despite being raised apart. His curiosity burned with a fundamental need to know more. And so five years ago, he'd written a brief letter to his birth mother, sent it to the adoption agency to be placed in his file, and put the search in motion.

CJ had freaked out. He'd only been seventeen then and they'd recently lost their parents; suddenly his older brother wanted to find his birth mother and twin. It had been too much for CJ. Samantha had thought that CJ was being a spoiled brat who would simply have to deal with it. Problem was, Jake had understood both sides. They'd both been right—CJ to feel… threatened, and Samantha to want to know how her future, how her children, might be affected by Jake. But after CJ had broken down one night, sobbing, unable to even speak, his grief, his fear speaking for itself, Jake had told Samantha now wasn't the time for him to find his birth mother, that maybe in six months, he could broach it again with CJ.

Samantha had flipped. *You're putting CJ first*, she'd shouted, pointing a long nail at his chest. *The man I marry will put me first*. She'd stormed out, and that was the last Jake had seen of her.

But his birth mother hadn't responded to the letter anyway—until just two months ago. Out of the clear blue sky on a rainy March afternoon, he'd received a call from a private investigator in Blue Gulch about how his birth mother had read his letter five years ago, was sorry for the long delay and hoped to make contact. At first Jake had said he wasn't interested and practically hung up on the investigator. But then his birth mother, Sarah Mack, had written him a short letter, assuring him that when he was ready she'd be there, and he'd been unable to stop thinking about her. Who she was, what the circumstances of his birth were, what she might know about his twin. And so he'd called Sarah Mack, who lived clear across Texas. Three meetings in Blue Gulch later, Jake had developed a real kinship with Sarah and with the quaint ranching town. And since Jake had been dealing with a bitter uncle who felt the Morrow family ranch should have passed on to him and was constantly filing lawsuits, Jake brought up the idea to CJ of just walking away and starting over in Blue Gulch; he'd seen a ranch for sale that had felt like home the minute he stepped on the land. CJ, who as usual had been dealing with an angry ex who liked to pass by with a rifle out her car window, had quietly agreed but had made it crystal clear that Jake's birth family wasn't a subject he wanted to talk about.

Sarah Mack had told him the only thing she knew about his twin was that they were fraternal. Thirty-two years ago, at a home for pregnant teenagers, she hadn't been able to hold either baby, let alone see them, but she'd overheard a nurse comment on it. She didn't know anything about who might have adopted him. There was nothing in the twins' file to indicate he wanted to make contact, but Sarah had left her own information for him. Lately, the idea of finding his twin was consuming Jake to the point he couldn't sleep at night.

Now he glanced over at CJ in the barn, his brother grinning while telling a dirty joke that had even shy Golden doubling over with laughter. Jake wasn't sure if he should start the search on the down low or talk to CJ about it first. Since his brother had agreed to move to where his birth mother lived, where her family lived, CJ had to have come around somewhat. But something told him his brother wouldn't be comfortable about Jake trying to make contact with his twin, even if CJ wasn't that grieving seventeen-year-old kid anymore.

"Speaking of dinner tonight, who's on duty to cook?" Jake asked Hank, gesturing at the other cowboys; CJ and Golden were checking on Frodo, the very old gelding Jake had rescued, while Golden cleaned up the barn for the night.

Hank pulled out the little notebook he carried everywhere. A folded up schedule of the month of May. "Tonight is CJ. Guess we're having burned burgers and charred beans."

Again. Except last night, on Golden's turn, the burgers were mostly raw and the beans hard as a rock. "I need to find us a cook," Jake said for the hundredth time. He'd put an ad in the local free weekly and stuck a notice up on the town green's bulletin board, but none of the applicants were right for the job, and Jake wasn't all that picky. Most had issues with the early morning breakfast hour, which was five sharp at the Full Circle, meaning arriving for work at four thirty before the birds were even awake. He'd added "live-in" to the ads, noting the job would come with room and board, but of the bunch who'd applied, two had turned up drunk for the interview and five had no cooking experience and couldn't even tell Jake how to make scrambled eggs. The last applicant, a woman with real experience as a sauté cook in the steak house in town, broke into tears during the interview and confessed she didn't really want the job—she only wanted to be close to CJ, who'd dumped her after two dates.

"Oh hell, I'll cook tonight," Jake said, craving a steak grilled just right, a baked potato with sour cream and chives, and cold, fresh salad with croutons and his favorite dressing, blue cheese. All that times five meant dinner would be a while, and he still had phone calls to return, invoices to pay and auction sites to look over for livestock.

He sent Hank to tell Golden, still a rookie, that he'd put Starlight's saddle backward on its stand, then turned toward the house and the kitchen. He had a mind to sneak into Hurley's Homestyle Kitchen tomorrow and offer to pay any one of their cooks double their salary to come work for him. But then he wouldn't be able to show his face there again, and he craved their po'boys too often for that. Plus, no one messed with Essie Hurley, who owned the place.

His phone buzzed with a text—from Fern, who'd sold him the goats earlier. *That flock of sheep we talked about? I'm selling it to the LoneStar Ranch instead. Their foreman doesn't tell me I smell like cow crap.*

Oh hell, he thought for the millionth time, shaking his head.

Emma Hurley had been through a trying time or two in her twenty-six years, but nothing compared to locating one very handsome, slippery cowboy who clearly did not want to be found. *Well, I finally did find you, Joshua Smith, and I'm coming whether you like it or not!*

She'd been trying to track down the guy for six weeks now, ever since she'd discovered she was pregnant. Once the shock had worn off she was filled with a deep-down happiness about the baby, but she still wondered how on earth she could have been so careless to sleep with a stranger—a ridiculously good-looking, smooth-talking stranger who'd said all the right things, including that of course he would use a condom. The condom had torn, apparently. If Joshua had noticed, he hadn't said anything. But maybe he had noticed. And maybe that was why he was gone without a word in the middle of the night, no note, no cell phone number, no nothing.

Once she knew she was pregnant, she tried to find him by asking around the rodeo circuit, where they'd met, but no one seemed to have heard of a rookie bull rider named Joshua Smith. Finally, another cowboy said he was pretty sure Joshua worked on a ranch in Blue Gulch, which had been a relief—Emma had family in that town, a great-aunt, Essie Hurley, who owned a popular restaurant, and three cousins. But after weeks in Blue Gulch, staying at Essie's and working part-time at Hurley's Homestyle Kitchen when it was clear Essie didn't need the help, Emma still hadn't tracked Joshua down.

Until this morning—when she'd been waiting on her iced mocha at the coffee shop and overheard two men talking about the rodeo as they were walking out. She'd asked them if they knew of a cowboy named Joshua Smith and she'd expected the usual, "No, sorry." But a funny look came over one of the men's faces and he said, "Joshua Smith? Do you mean Tex? Bull rider, right?"

Emma had almost dropped the iced mocha the barista had handed her. Apparently, Joshua had recently gotten a job at the Full Circle ranch ten miles

out of town and only went by Tex. He probably
switched to his given name for women he wanted to
seduce. Joshua Smith sounded like a man who'd be
there in the morning; Tex, more like a good-time guy.
Nevertheless. She'd found him!

Now, as she followed the directions her great-aunt
had given her to the ranch, she thought about how
easy it had been for Joshua—Tex—to fool her. The
day she'd met him, back in late January, she'd had a
whopper of an argument with her father, a CEO whose
photo should appear beside the dictionary definition
of the word *controlling*. Reginald Hurley was upset
that she wouldn't quit her job as a short-order cook
in an all-night diner, a place she loved working, with
coworkers she adored and a manager who liked coming up with funny names for the specials. *You'll never
meet an appropriate man in a greasy spoon like that,
Emma,* her father always said. *Let me get you a job at
Le Vieux—it's a four-star restaurant.*

Emma had tried that already; after culinary school
she'd worked in three fancy restaurants. In one, the
chef screamed in her ear to the point she'd drop ex-
pensive cuts of meat. In another, the sous-chef would
slap her on the butt everytime he passed her, then lied
about her work performance when she reported him to
the owner. In the final one, a customer had sent back
his salmon three times; it wasn't "just right" and he
couldn't explain why, and she'd been fired on the spot.
The next day she'd seen the help-wanted sign in the
diner, noticed that the cooks visible through the open
area behind the counter were whistling and chatting
away, and she'd gone right in. The manager liked to
give awards to the staff to keep them happy. She'd

won Best Burger, Best Flapjacks and Best Attitude on Busy Sunday Mornings.

She'd tried to explain to her father that she wasn't necessarily looking for a man or a husband; she had a dream of becoming a personal chef but wanted more experience first and loved the diner, where she made comfort food and smiley face meals for kids. His response? *Frankly, Emma, it's embarrassing that you work in that dump. It's bad enough you live in an apartment above a pizzeria. Come on.*

After that argument, she'd taken herself to the rodeo to lose herself in an afternoon of watching hunky cowboys in action, only to be sweet-talked by the hunkiest about being true to herself and living her own life and no one else's. She'd said yes to an impromptu invitation of dinner and slow dancing with the blue-eyed cowboy. They'd talked and talked and talked through dinner, looked deeply into each other's eyes as they'd danced, and then they were holding hands and kissing their way to her hotel room, where she forgot everything that had been troubling her. When the dawn woke her up, her cowboy was gone and Emma had lain there wondering if she'd daydreamed the whole thing. Six weeks later, when a pink plus sign appeared in the home pregnancy test window, she knew she hadn't.

Emma drove on, thinking about what she was going to say to Joshua. *I just wanted you to know. I don't expect anything from you.* And she'd see what he said.

A few feet up on the left, near a big weeping willow, just like Aunt Essie—who Emma had confided in— said to look for, was a sign for the Full Circle Ranch. She turned and headed down the drive, tall oaks lining her path, the green canopy of leaves barely letting through the bright May sunshine, going strong close to six o'clock in the evening.

Up ahead she could see a stately house, almost a Colonial style with white pillars and a red door, the same red that matched the big barn behind it and another farther down. There were pastures as far as the eye could see, some containing bulls, some smaller areas with goats and sheep. Two cats were chasing after something flying low, a butterfly, maybe, until a black goat suddenly booked out of the barn, headed west. Suddenly, the cats flew behind the barn and the front door of the house opened.

A tall, dark-haired man in his early thirties, wearing a white apron and carrying a pair of silver tongs, rushed out, a cell phone to his ear, a piece of paper in his other hand. His gaze was on the runaway goat.

"Oh hell," she heard him mutter as she pulled up. "No, not you, Anderson," he said into the phone. "Yes, I want the three heifers. Friday's fine." He pocketed the phone. "CJ!" he called out.

Emma glanced around. A younger man, with a shock of glossy dark hair, came out of the house behind him.

"I'm texting Stella," the younger guy said. "Can it wait?"

"Do you think Goatby can wait?" he asked, pointing at the goat halfway across the open field.

"Oh hell," CJ said, and Emma had to smile. He'd said it just like the man in the apron had.

Emma stepped from the car, the scent of burned meat in the air. "Is something burning?" she asked the man. He was tall, at least six foot two, with dark brown hair and green eyes, and muscular and handsome in the way of the old Westerns her grandmother used to watch on TV when Emma was young. That combined with the apron and tongs made her smile.

"Oh hell!" he grumbled. He pivoted, but then turned toward the guy chasing the goat, then turned back toward the house. "I've got five steaks on the grill out back." He threw up his hands, clearly torn between chasing after the goat and saving dinner.

She'd waited six weeks to tell Joshua that she was pregnant with his baby; she could wait another ten minutes to ask for him. "I'll take care of the steaks. I'm a cook at Hurley's. Go get Goatby."

He stared at her, his eyes crinkling in confusion, and then he shook his head as if to clear it and raced after the younger guy and the goat. She could hear it bleating.

Emma followed the scent of the burning steaks into a large kitchen with gorgeous gray cabinets and stainless steel appliances, and then out through the open sliding glass doors to a patio that led to a big backyard. An orange cat was curled up under a shady tree, its eyes slitting open for a brief look at the visitor.

The steaks still smelled good, which meant they might be salvageable. If it's one thing her great-aunt Essie had taught her: a good barbecue sauce could save just about anything.

She found another pair of tongs and turned the steaks. Was this a family dinner? She had no idea. Back inside the kitchen she peeked inside the oven and saw five potatoes baking in foil; a timer was ticking with two minutes to go. She gave one of the potatoes a gentle squeeze, then took off the foil and chucked it, brushed olive oil on the skins and set the timer for ten more minutes. There were the makings for salad on the counter. A head of romaine lettuce, a cucumber, two tomatoes. She opened the refrigerator and found a store-bought blue cheese dressing. She gave it a little taste. Not bad, but nothing compared to her aunt Essie's homemade dressings.

By the time the oven timer dinged, she had the dining room table set for five, the salad tossed in a big silver bowl, and butter and sour cream and chives on a serving tray awaiting the potatoes. She headed out to the patio with a platter for the steaks. Perfect. The slight char on one side would just make them that much better. She found some sauces in the refrigerator and set them out too.

She heard voices and looked out the dining room window. The man in the apron and the younger guy were heading back with the goat. She smiled at Goatby, who looked quite pleased with himself and his little escapade. Three other men, of various ages and all in cowboy hats and jeans, were coming from one of the other barns.

She stepped outside. "Dinner's on the table."

The five men stopped and stared at her. The one in the apron said, "Dinner's on the table?"

"Sure is," she said. "Come see for yourselves. I wasn't sure what y'all wanted to drink so I set out the beer and the pitcher of iced tea."

He stared at her, then switched the tongs from his right hand to his left. "Jake Morrow," he said, stretching out his right hand.

She shook it. "Emma Hurley."

The men followed her into the dining room. She

heard someone whisper, "She's a Hurley, and all Hurleys can cook."

"Hank," Jake said, stopping in front of the table. "Do you see what I see or is this some kind of mirage?"

"Oh, I see it," said the fortyish one with the thick red hair. "I don't believe it, but I see it."

The eldest one, with the wild gray-brown hair and beard, added, "Me too, Boss."

Emma smiled at them. "Sit and eat before it all gets cold."

They sat down, stared at the food for a moment, then grabbed at sauces and filled their glasses with beer or iced tea.

"Are you some kind of fairy godcook?" Jake asked, taking a bite of the steak. "I thought these were goners."

She laughed. "Does wonders for my ego to hear."

"Please, sit down," Jake said to her. He went to the sidebar and got a plate, then cut his steak in half, split his potato and handed her the plate. "Least I can do."

That sure was nice. "Thanks. I'm starving."

"Hey, Jake, I thought you said no one had answered the ad for a cook since the last fake who was really one of CJ's broken hearts," said the eldest of the five men, the tall, large one with the unruly hair and beard.

CJ shot the older man a glare with his very blue eyes.

Jake took a bite of salad. "No one has."

"Then where did this gorgeous creature come from?" CJ said, sliding a killer smile over to her.

She ignored the faux flattery and swiped her bite of potato in sour cream. "I'm staying with my great-aunt Essie—she owns Hurley's Homestyle Kitchen in town. Know of it?"

Jake smiled. "Know of it? We're there half the week."

"I work in the kitchen part-time," she said, then took a sip of her iced tea. "But the reason I'm here is that I heard a cowboy named Joshua—Tex—works at the Full Circle. I've come to see him on personal business."

Every one of the men stopped eating. Stopped talking. They looked at one another, then at her.

"Miss—ma'am," Jake said. He cleared his throat. "I'm sorry, but Tex had an accident about three weeks ago. He didn't survive."

She felt the blood drain from her face. She opened her mouth to speak but nothing came out.

She felt Jake's hand on her shoulder. "Miss?"

She closed her eyes and put down her fork. "Oh." That was all she could manage.

"Was Tex a friend of yours?" another of the men asked. "I'm Grizzle. We're the crew here at the ranch," he added, gesturing at the guys at the table. "We all became great buddies with Tex, even though we'd only been working here together for about a week when he died."

"I'm Hank Timber," said the redhead with a nod at her. "The foreman at the Full Circle." He tilted his head and stared at her. "His death left us dumbstruck too back when it happened."

"I'm pregnant with his baby," she blurted out. Five set of eyes stared at her, a few open jaws. She hadn't meant to say it, but it just came out. "I've been looking for him ever since I found out. We met at the rodeo in Stockton in January, but then…lost touch. When I found out I was pregnant, I tried to track him down but I only knew his given name."

"Joshua Smith," Jake said. He had a look of reverence in his expression that told her he'd gotten close to Joshua too. Based on how close she'd felt to the guy in one night, she could imagine how these men had felt after even just a week of working long days together on a ranch.

The cowboys ate quickly, then all nodded at her, said they were "real sorry for her loss," and practically ran from the dining room, leaving her and Jake Morrow.

The foreman, Hank, came back. "Sorry for the baby's loss too. That's real sad." Then he turned back and hurried from the room.

Jake turned to her, his green eyes full of sympathy. "I own the Full Circle. That was the entire crew, including my brother CJ. He's the one who helped me bring back the goat. Tex—Joshua—was one of the hands and we all liked him a lot. He was an old soul and wise for his age, all of twenty-seven. Even though his nickname was Tex, Grizzle referred to him as Owl."

She found herself unable to speak again. She hadn't even been sure what to expect when she would finally lock eyes with Joshua again and tell him she was expecting his baby. She'd been pretty sure he'd run for the hills, disappear the way he had after their one great night together. But part of her thought he wouldn't, that he'd at least say, "Okay, this baby is my responsibility, and I don't duck out on that." Of course, now she'd never know.

Jake stared at her for a moment. "He talked about you." He seemed to be remembering something, then nodded. "One morning he was preoccupied, and that wasn't Tex's way. He finally told us he'd sneaked out on a woman in the middle of the night without leaving his name or a number and that he couldn't stop thinking about her. He'd said if he'd been a settling down guy, he would have chosen that 'smart, interesting woman with the honey-colored hair and the biggest blue eyes he'd ever seen.' That was exactly how he put it."

Emma did have honey-colored hair, or so Joshua had referred to it many times the night he'd run his fingers through it. And she did have big blue eyes, like her mother's. So he must have been talking about her. She appreciated the "smart" and "interesting." Plus the timing was right.

And now the rancher knew every detail of her failed romance with Joshua Smith.

"I'm very sorry," Jake said again. He seemed about to say something, but then took a gulp of beer.

Now it was her turn to say "oh hell," except the two words just kept echoing in her head. Along with *Now what?*

She didn't want to leave. She still had her apartment a town over in Oak Creek, but her lease was ending this month anyway, and when she thought of Oak Creek she thought of her father and how he'd reacted when she told him she was pregnant, that she was keeping the baby and, yes, she knew who the father was but not where, exactly.

Oh for God's sake, Emma, Reginald Hurley had said. *Now you've really done it. A baby out of wedlock.*

What the hell will people think? He'd shaken his head, a few times for good measure, then had added, *I'll start a list of colleagues who might come to your rescue. Of course, most will be a bit lacking in some area or another to take on a pregnant woman. But they'll all be solvent and ambitious. I'll set up some dates for you and I'm sure you'll hit it off with one of them.*

She'd packed her bags and left town an hour later, feeling more alone than ever, then had settled in Blue Gulch, grateful for kind relatives nearby, sure she'd find Tex soon. Her father had called a few times, bellowing into the phone that she'd lose her window for the blind dates—once she lost her figure, forget it. She'd told her father in no uncertain terms that she would not be going on any of his husband dates and was staying in Blue Gulch, at least until she found Joshua. *Appalling*, he'd said. *Chasing after some two-bit rodeo loser who ran off on you.* That was three weeks ago. A week ago, in a kinder but still demanding, controlling tone: *Emma, come home already. You'll move in and we'll fix up the guest room for a nursery. At least I can assure my grandchild will want for nothing.* She'd forced herself to thank her dad for the offer, but had told him she was staying put.

She wasn't going back to Oak Creek. And she couldn't put her finger on it, but there was something in how her baby's father had lived and worked here, spent his final moment on this land, among friends, that made her want to stay. And somehow, she felt at home at the Full Circle, maybe because she'd fixed dinner and had eaten with the crew, who all seemed like nice people. And she liked this Jake Morrow, who'd told her with real sympathy in his voice that Joshua had passed away.

"Jake, I could use a job and a place to live. I could learn how to be a cowgirl, take over Joshua's job." Even when she was six or nine months pregnant she could certainly lead cattle out to pasture and groom the horses.

He stared at her. "You're looking for a job?" A smile lit his face. God, he was handsome when he smiled. "What I really need is a cook for me and the guys. When you said you worked at Hurley's, I thought I must be dreaming since I've been saying I need a cook for weeks and suddenly, you turn up and not only save dinner but serve the best meal I've had in a long time."

"Well, thank you for that. I've been a cook for years. Most Saturday mornings at the diner in Oak Creek I was averaging seventy-five pancakes and cracking a hundred eggs an hour. I can definitely handle five hungry cowboys."

Relief was evident on Jake's face. "The job comes with room and board, plus a salary." Her eyes widened at the pay he mentioned. Three times better than her hourly wages at the diner. "This house is plenty big. I live here with CJ—our rooms are on the second floor—and there's a third floor that will be all yours. It has a sitting area, good-sized bedroom and a bathroom with a spa tub."

Perfect. Her aunt would be relieved that she'd found a just-right-for-her job and home. The Victorian that housed Hurley's Homestyle Kitchen was large, and only Essie and her two black lab puppies lived there but, unfortunately, Emma was allergic to dogs. Considering that Emma hadn't sneezed once since arriving at the Full Circle, there likely wasn't a dog around. That would be unusual for a ranch, so maybe dog allergies were something she and Jake Morrow had in common.

Jake took another sip of his beer. "The job involves serving breakfast—and these guys like their morning chow—at five sharp so we can starting chores at five thirty, fixings for a cold lunch that we can serve ourselves whenever we're ready to take a break, and then a hot dinner at 5:30 p.m. Sound good?"

"Sounds *great*. I work for my aunt two days a week, just the lunch shift. This way I can keep that." She didn't want to give up the lunch shift at Hurley's. The past few weeks she'd loved getting to know her great-aunt and cousins and their families. She loved the idea of raising her baby in a town where he or she would have a lot of family close by.

"Then we have ourselves a deal," Jake said, the waning sun glinting through the window on his tanned forearms. "Start tomorrow morning?"

They shook on it, the feel of his warm, strong hand such a surprising comfort she didn't want to let go. That was unexpected. She forced her gaze away from his kind, curious green eyes.

She wasn't about to let herself fall for another man, no matter how seemingly kind and chivalrous when kind and chivalrous was a comfort. She was determined to make her own way, to not need anyone, to be self-sufficient and a good mother. She already knew she was a good cook. Right now, she'd spend her spare time reading her book on baby development and saving up money for onesies and bottles and diapers, not to mention a bassinet and all the other baby things her little one would need.

She could and would stand on her own two feet.

Chapter Two

Jake was wide-awake at 4:35 a.m, ten minutes before his alarm was set to go off. Usually he'd have to
peel his eyes open and force himself out of his very
comfortable king-size bed with the amazing down-
filled pillows CJ had bought him last Christmas. This
morning, though, well before the crack of dawn, Jake
wanted to check on his new cook and make sure she
was all right.

He couldn't stop thinking about her last night. One
flight up, alone in a strange house, maybe tossing and
turning with the news that her baby's father had passed
away, that she was pregnant and on her own. He'd
thought about going upstairs and gently knocking on
her door, asking if she needed anything, if the quilt
was too heavy or if she wanted a pitcher of water,
but he had a feeling that he should leave her be with

her thoughts. She'd come to the ranch to find her baby's father, and Jake had dropped a bombshell on her. Twice he'd almost gotten out of bed to check on her, and twice he'd made himself stay put. He hated the idea of her by herself in her room, but Jake was practically a stranger. And her boss.

After dinner last night, she'd driven to her aunt's house to get her bags and he'd sat outside on the porch with Redford, the only of his three cats who liked coming in the house. When her car had pulled back in an hour later, a strange relief had come over him. He still wasn't sure what that was about. He felt responsible for her, maybe. He'd rushed over to her car to take her bags, just one suitcase and a tote, and as she walked next to him, he'd been so aware of her. Emma Hurley was tall, at least five foot nine, but there was an ethereal quality to her, despite the determination he could see clearly in her eyes. He could tell she was a strong woman.

He'd shown her around the third floor, which seemed to be to her liking. While she'd been gone, he'd stocked her shower with soap and shampoo and conditioner and hung fresh towels on the racks. Then he'd given her the tour of the rest of the house, the enormous living room with its massive stone fireplace, his office adjacent, the dining room and kitchen, both of which she was familiar with. From the living room he pointed out the two doors visible on the second-floor landing, one at each end of the long hall. His bedroom was on the left and CJ's on the right.

Then he'd shown her around the huge kitchen, where the pots and pans were, the cooking utensils, the silverware. She'd turned down his offer of a cup of herbal tea, which his weekly house cleaner had brought over, and said she'd just like to turn in since she'd be up early in the morning.

He'd wanted to say something about Tex, that he was sorry, again, but there was something in her expression, something private, that had him just saying, *Well, good night, see you at five*, and heading back to his office.

Now he got out of bed, took a quick, hot shower and dressed in his work clothes, jeans, a long-sleeved T-shirt and his brown boots and headed downstairs by four forty-five. Were those voices he heard coming from the kitchen or was Emma listening to the radio? The closer he got, he could swear he heard Hank's voice. And his brother's. And was that Golden who said he liked plain pancakes while Grizzle said pancakes without blueberries were just boring old flapjacks. The guys were never early for breakfast.

He entered the kitchen to find Golden stirring pancake batter, Grizzle washing the containers of blueberries and strawberries, and his brother cracking eggs and scrambling them in a big silver mixing bowl. Hank was frying bacon on the big griddle. And Emma, the new cook, was sitting down at the round café table by the window, sipping something from a red mug, his cat Redford at her feet.

What the heck was going on?

"Hey, Boss," Hank said, using tongs to flip over each piece of bacon.

Emma stood up, her cheeks a bit pink, her long golden-brown ponytail swaying a bit. "I came in at four thirty to find them already cooking breakfast. They wouldn't let me do a thing."

"Least we can do," Grizzle said, offering Emma a smile.

"Least," Golden added, nodding at her, his blond bangs flopping on his forehead.

"Emma, pass me that platter, please," CJ said without a hint of his usual flirtation in his voice.

Huh. Not only were his crew acting like actual gentlemen, including his brother, they weren't saying stupid stuff or trying to impress her and instead insulting her with either flat-out stupidity or sexual innuendos. And after last night's delicious dinner— even the baked potatoes tasted a thousand times better than usual—they knew they'd be in for a great breakfast this morning, but had given that up to cook themselves. Now they'd have the usual overcooked pancakes and rubbery eggs and hard-as-rocks home fries with too much pepper.

He smiled. He might not have worked very long with his crew, well, except for CJ, but he'd known the minute he'd met the say-the-wrong-thing Hank, the rough-around-the-edges Grizzle, and the can-barely-look-you-in-the eye Golden that they could be trusted, that they'd work hard, that under all the quirks were damned good men. He'd been right.

And he had a feeling he knew why the ragtag bunch was so comfortable around Emma and falling over themselves to be kind to her. Emma was not only pregnant and therefore off-limits—because none of the cowboys thought themselves remotely father material—but she'd been "done wrong" by Tex, by one of them.

"It's good of you all to help," Jake said to the guys. "I'll put myself on toast duty." He headed to the counter, where the bread boxes were full of bread and English muffins and bagels, and toasted up a couple of each, then grabbed butter and cream cheese from the refrigerator and brought it all out to the dining room. The table was already set. The silverware was in the wrong places and half the forks were upside down, which meant Golden or Grizzle had set the table. He smiled. He knew he had a great crew.

Once they were all seated, eating and drinking coffee and orange juice, Hank asked Emma if she had a name picked out for the baby.

She paused, a forkful of very well-done scrambled eggs in her hand. "Well, if she's a girl, I'm thinking Violet after my mother. I'm not sure about a boy's name yet." She frowned, glancing down at her plate. "I always figured I'd name my firstborn son after my father, but—" She stopped and quickly ate her bite of eggs, then pushed the rest around on her plate with her fork.

"But your father's in prison now?" Hank asked, slathering cream cheese on a bagel half.

Emma looked confused. "What? No. He's not in prison. He's…he's just… "

"A real jerk?" Grizzle offered.

Emma bit her lip. "Well, he's just… "

Jake glanced at her. He's just not living up to being a namesake was what he suspected the issue was.

A phone pinged, saving Emma from answering. CJ pulled his cell out of his pocket and looked at it, then rolled his eyes and put it away.

"Who's mad at you now?" Hank asked him with a grin. "Yesterday you were hot on Stella. Today, you're done with her, is that right?"

"Don't gossip about Stella," CJ said, his blue eyes flashing. "It's not right."

"Whoa, what's this?" Grizzle said, his face lighting up with a potential taunt. "CJ Morrow defending a young lady's honor?"

"He must like this one," Hank said.

"Stella who works at the bookstore?" Golden asked, eyeing CJ, who nodded. "She's really nice." He cleared his throat and looked around the table as if to see if anyone was paying attention to him. Jake had a feeling that Golden had grown up being ignored. "The other day I went to the bookstore to buy my dad a birthday present, but I couldn't figure out what to get him. Stella asked me a bunch of questions about what he liked and suggested a biography of the first FBI director. My dad loved it."

For Golden to pipe up, particularly to that extent, this Stella *had* to be nice.

Jake stared at his brother. CJ's head was down as he pretended great interest in forking up his home fries. Interesting. Maybe his brother did like Stella—for more than the usual three days.

Talk turned to what needed doing that morning—from the usual daily chores to a fence that had to be mended up near the ridge, to moving the bulls out to a new pasture, to taking a trip into town for some supplies at the feed store. The crew had eaten their fill, but instead of getting up and heading out, leaving whoever was on cooking duty to clean up, as was the usual routine, they all started picking up their plates.

Emma stood up. "No, no! You all have done so much for me this morning and I appreciate it. I'm the cook here now and I didn't even lift a finger this morning. So I will clean up, as I will every meal. I may be pregnant, but I'm capable of not only cooking, but lifting plates." She smiled at them. "Go ahead. And thank you, guys. All of you. You sure know how to make a lady feel welcome."

At that last sentence, Jake almost gasped. Grizzle actually took off his hat and held it to his chest. Hank's chest puffed up. Golden had pink circles on his cheeks. And CJ threw an aw-shucks smile at Emma but a second later was glued to his phone as if waiting for a text that wasn't coming.

Once the crew headed out, Jake had to force himself not to help clear the table. Emma was capable and he didn't want to seem overly protective.

He finished his coffee. "I don't know how you managed it, but you actually have the guys almost acting like gentlemen. They're pretty rough around the edges—even CJ, who thinks he's Mr. Smooth. They're all looking for love, but they kind of repel women. Especially the ones they're most interested in. There's a dance tonight they're all going to—maybe over dinner you could give them some tips on what they're doing wrong."

She stacked breakfast dishes along her arm. "I'll try, but honestly, I'm O for three in the romance department myself. I mean, here I am, pregnant and single. Who am I to give advice to anyone about love?" She smiled, her pretty face lighting up for a moment, but then she paused and her expression changed as though she was thinking about something. She grabbed the butter dish with her free hand and headed toward the kitchen.

He followed with his mug, needing a refill on the

strong coffee. "You got Grizzle to take off his hat indoors without even asking him to. That's how good you are without even working at it."

"He did, didn't he?" She smiled again. "I'll see what I can do."

He wanted to stay and talk to her. Ask her about her father. Ask her more about where she was from in Oak Creek, if she grew up on a ranch. But as he watched her set the dishes on the counter, the sunrise glowing past her through the sliding glass door to the kitchen, he was socked with such a pang of attraction that he backed away. What the hell was this?

Yes, Emma was pretty. And kind. And...vulnerable. Last night, Jake had found himself tossing and turning with the notion that he was responsible for Emma's baby. Tex had been riding one of the new mares and a backfiring truck spooked the horse and threw him.

He turned away, his chest tightening with his line of thought. Maybe he wasn't attracted so much as that he felt responsible for her. Tex had been a nice guy, his employee, and Jake felt like he owed Emma something.

Which was fine. He'd take responsibility. He'd given her a job and a home, and he'd furnish a nursery for her baby and make sure the child had everything he or she needed, including a fund started for college.

Now that he'd settled that in his head, a million other thoughts bombarded him—from livestock he wanted to buy for the ranch to Frodo the old black horse on the mend in the barn, to...his twin brother, who was walking around out there, maybe looking for him. Jake needed to talk to CJ, let him know he was thinking about getting the search started in earnest. Jake would assure his brother that nothing would ever come between them, that he'd never feel any differently, that he'd always have time for his kid brother. No matter what. Which was all true.

So why was he putting it off? CJ wasn't that same kid who'd sobbed in his arms five years ago about losing everything. He was a man. So why was Jake so reluctant to bring up the subject again?

It wasn't like him to be unsure of how to proceed, to not know the best way to go with something. Dammit, this thing had him out of sorts. Aware that Emma seemed to be watching him while she loaded the dishwasher, he nodded at her, thanked her again for breakfast and headed out, stopping to watch the sun rise over the ridge. He focused on it, trying to clear his mind. But just when his mind settled he started thinking about the beautiful woman in his house. He *was* attracted to her in a way he hadn't been to any woman in five years.

Well, he'd have to add himself to his lineup of clueless cowboys because no matter what he told the guys about the heart wanting what it wants, he wasn't about to heed his own.

The dishwasher full and going, the dining room table clean and the kitchen spotless, Emma glanced in the refrigerator to see what the guys would have for lunch, which was "make your own." There were at least five pounds of sliced meats, from roast beef to ham to turkey, plus condiments and lettuce and tomatoes. Someone sure liked potato salad—there were two one-pound take-out containers from Hurley's Homestyle Kitchen. And was that a jar of pickled herring? On the counter, one of a few bread boxes was full of Kaiser rolls. Whoever did the grocery shopping knew what he was doing. The fruit bowls were picked almost clean through, so those would need replenishing. Emma would have to ask Jake if she should take on the shopping.

She headed up to her room on the third floor, her suite like a palace compared to her small apartment in Oak Creek, if not the big house she'd grown up in. She loved the old hardwood floors in her bedroom here at the Full Circle, the soft Persian carpet covering a good portion of it. Her bed was plush, just the way she liked it, and the views outside all the windows were of endless green and trees and livestock. She glanced in the corner between the two big windows. That's where she'd put the crib when it was time.

She touched her hand to her belly, amazed for the millionth time that in just five months she'd have a baby. Emma had lost her mother her senior year of high school and wished Violet Hurley were here. What a grandmother she would be. Her dad's disappointed face came to mind and she thought about calling him to let him know about her baby's father and where she was living now. But he'd just insist she come home and not listen to a word about how *she* felt, what *she* wanted, so she kept her phone in her pocket.

After a quick shower, Emma dressed in jeans and a pale blue T-shirt for her shift at Hurley's. She helped out on Tuesdays—always a busy day since the restaurant was closed Monday and folks missed their po'boys and ribs and chicken fried steak—and Saturdays, today, the busiest lunch day. She headed back downstairs, gave Redford a scratch on the head and went out the front door. She could see Hank and Golden carrying hay bales from the barn, and in one of the pastures, Grizzle and CJ were leading the bulls farther out. She wondered where Jake was, what he was doing.

A few weeks ago, her baby's father had been out there on this land. She touched her hand to her stomach again and let the warm May breeze wrap around her. She suddenly wanted to see the ranch and take a look in the outbuildings.

The big red barn was huge, home to many stalls with horses and a bunch of goats and sheep. She saw Jake checking on a small herd of goats in their pen and watched him open the gate and let them into the fenced-in pasture. The morning sun lit up his dark hair and shone on his strong, handsome profile. She realized she was staring and forced her gaze to the large bulletin board on the wall by the double doors.

"Bucks' Choice Dance?" Emma said, reading the flyer announcing a dance for the rancher association fund-raiser being held that night.

"The crew has really been looking forward to this one," Jake said, adjusting his brown Stetson. "Every song, the men get to choose their partner and it's considered ill manners to say no. Last month it was ladies' choice."

"CJ was brand-new in town and didn't get to sit down once," Hank said, scanning the clipboard in his hand. "Boy, was he tired the next morning."

Emma smiled. She wondered if Jake had gone and danced the night way. "And it says here since it's

bucks' choice, men pay the ten-dollar admission but
ladies go in free."

Grizzle led in a pretty brown-and-white mare to
the grooming area and unbridled her. "But men *drink*
free, whereas ladies have to pay."

"Which they gladly will since they have to dance
with whoever asks, unless the guy's a creep or an ex,"
Hank said, checking something off on his clipboard.

"Wait," Emma said. "You're saying women not only
have to dance with whoever asks, but they have to pay
for their drinks too?"

Hank nodded. "Ain't that grand? It switches every
month, so it works out." He chuckled, then turned to
Jake. "You're going, right, Boss?"

"Me?" Jake asked, closing the goats' pen. "No. I
hung up my dancing shoes."

"You're single, aincha?" Grizzle said as he removed
the mare's saddle and pad.

"Yeah, but—" Jake began.

"Plus, you're a member of the rancher's association.
You *have* to go," Hank pointed out. "Or you can forget
about becoming a board member. Trust me, I know."

Grizzle frowned. "I hate tab keepers."

"Way of the world," Hank said. "Oh, and, Grizz. Do
your dance partners a favor—shave before the event.
The barber shop's open till six tonight."

"I ain't cutting my hair and shaving this beard,"
Grizzle muttered.

The foreman stared at him. "Are you forgetting
how that little girl jumped when she saw you at the
feed store? When you start to scare small children,
it's time for a shave and a haircut."

Grizzle waved his hand dismissively and stared

Hank down. "I'm sure you've got stuff to do. And considering you told a lady she smelled like cow dung, I don't think I should be taking pointers from you."

Hank's cheeks flamed. "Well, she did smell kind of like cow dung. So did I. We're ranchers, for Pete's sake."

Emma had a feeling these two could go at it for hours, but would be right there if one needed the other. And she wondered what Jake's "yeah, but" was about. *Yeah, but I'm dating someone and we're serious and she can't go tonight so I can't, either.* She sure hoped that wasn't it.

"I heard the association fund-raisers are dress up," Jake said. "That true?"

Hank nodded. "There'll be a line at Joe's all day. He's the barber in town. Has a place right on Main Street next to the drugstore. Can't miss it with the spinning red-and-white pole outside."

"I'll bet you'd look very handsome with a haircut and beard trim," Emma said to Grizzle.

"Then I guess I won't be going," Grizzle griped. He dropped the sponge he'd been using to wash the mare's neck into the bucket, then dried her off and led her to her stall.

Emma's face fell. "What's that about?" she whispered.

Jake shrugged. "Not sure."

"Maybe he's used to looking like a mountain man," Hank said. "You get used to your ways and then you can't imagine changing. Like Michelle, the librarian. She hasn't changed her look since high school and that was 1994. She has bigger shoulders than I do."

Emma glanced down toward the mare's stall. She

couldn't see Grizzle from where she was standing by the bulletin board. She looked at Jake, then headed over to the stall, where Grizzle was checking the mare's hooves. "I'm sorry about poking my nose into your business, Grizzle. That wasn't fair of me."

Grizzle glanced up. "Oh, no worries. Way I see it, if women don't like how I look, they're not the ones for me."

She smiled. "That's actually a very good philosophy."

He checked the hind hooves. "Of course, the few women who've turned my head since my wife died don't like the way I look. Michelle, the librarian Hank was talking about? I asked her to lunch a couple weeks back and she said yes, but when I picked her up she marched up to my truck and said she expected I'd at least clean up some and she couldn't very well go to lunch with me looking like I just came off a mountain after fifteen years. She went right back in her house."

Huh. That must have made Grizzle feel awful. But the man really did need a haircut. The wild gray-brown hair was long, wiry and stuck up in every direction, and the beard did the same.

He stared off into the middle distance for a moment, then sighed and dropped down on the stool at the back of the stall. "You want to know the last time I cut my hair and shaved and wore a suit and tie?"

"Yes," Emma said.

"My wife's funeral. Hell, I don't ever want to look like that again. I don't ever want to be reminded of that day." His face tightened and he stared down at the hay on the floor.

Oh, Grizzle. "I understand. The day my mother

died, my hair was in a braid and I was wearing sparkly blue nail polish. I've not been able to braid my hair or wear blue polish since." Violet Hurley's lovely face came to mind and she missed her mother so fiercely, again wishing more than anything she were there. "I definitely understand the sentiment. Being reminded of who you were on a particular day."

Grizzle glanced up at her, nodded, then let out a breath. "It's not like anyone could hold a candle to Liza, anyway. I don't know why I bother."

"Well, no one will ever be Liza, but someone will light up your heart regardless. You asked out the librarian for a reason. You must find her attractive."

He shrugged. "Only reason I asked her out is that she's tall, like me. Tallest woman in Blue Gulch. You're tall, and she's got three or four inches on you. I'm six-four."

Emma laughed. "Well, maybe you'll meet another tall woman at the dance. Someone who has other attributes you find appealing too."

He shrugged. "Not if I don't clean up, though. No one will even give me a chance."

"Well, maybe there's a compromise. A comb instead of scissors. A little hair gel. You could just trim your beard a bit too."

Grizzle let out quite a snort. "Me with hair gunk? CJ would laugh his head off."

"Have you seen the amount of hair product in CJ's hair?" Emma whispered with a grin.

Grizzle chuckled. "Well, maybe. Will you come by the bunkhouse 'bout an hour before the dance and help me?"

"I sure will," she promised.

"Oh, and, Emma?" Grizzle called as she was leaving. "I don't actually have a comb. I don't think Hank or Golden will let me borrow theirs."

Emma smiled. "I'll pick one up for you at the drugstore today. I'm going into town for my shift at Hurley's anyway."

He nodded at her, and she headed outside. Jake was standing near the open barn doors at the other end, just on the other side of the stall where she'd been talking to Grizzle. He was signing off on papers a man she didn't recognize was handing him. The guy got into his truck and drove off, and that's when she noticed the stack of hay bales on the other side of Jake. Hay delivery. She wondered if Jake had heard their conversation. She wasn't sure if Grizzle would like that.

"Jake?" she said. "I need to head to Hurley's for my lunch shift, and I thought I'd do the grocery shopping after. You're very low on fruit. And based on last night and this morning, the fridge and cupboards won't last more than another couple of days. Could you give me the basics on what everyone likes and if there are any allergies?"

"No picky eaters or allergies among us," Jake said. "We all pretty much like good basic home cooking. Meat and potatoes, chicken, pasta, fish. Big sandwiches for lunch. The usual for breakfast. The guys love their chips and pretzels."

"Got it," Emma said with a smile.

"We also all agree on pie, any kind," Hank added, coming from the barn. "And chocolate chip cookies, the crunchy kind."

She smiled again. "On my list. Well, see you at dinner." She glanced at Jake and found she couldn't take her eyes off him. Dammit. Why was she so drawn to him? The man was good-looking, yes. But it was more than that; there was something about him that made her feel...she didn't even know. Made her feel *what*?

Stop staring at the man and get in your car, she ordered herself. She could feel Hank eyeballing her, and given how Hank did seem to catch most things, except his own gaffes when it came to dealing with Fern, apparently, she didn't want the foreman to think she had a crush on the boss. She hurried to her car and got in. She lowered the windows to let in the gorgeous fresh country air.

Jake jogged over and leaned down, bracing those strong forearms on the window. "Grizzle okay?"

Hmm. Maybe he hadn't been listening to their conversation. Or maybe he just didn't want her to think he'd been eavesdropping. Regardless, she loved how much they all seemed to care about one another, despite the ribbing. "He's letting me at him with a comb before the dance."

Jake grinned. "Good work. Again."

She grinned back. "So I suppose you'll have to go to the dance, after all, given what Hank said about supporting the rancher's association."

He groaned. "Well, since it's bucks' choice, I have the choice of not asking *anyone* to dance."

"I hear ya," she said. "No thanks. Dances lead to dates lead to kisses lead to more dates lead to relationships and heartache."

One dark eyebrow raised. "That's exactly right."

So why was she suddenly imagining herself in his

arms for one sensuous slow dance, his hands on her waist, his body so close she could smell his shampoo?

And why did she like the idea of Jake not asking anyone to dance?

Chapter Three

Jake watched Emma's small silver car disappear up the long drive, and then he headed back to the house to answer calls and look at more auction sites, his mind on the idea of his beautiful new cook in his arms for a slow dance. Would not be happening. As he'd told her, he might have to go to the dance, but that didn't mean he had to ask anyone to dance. And he doubted she'd go, either, based on what she'd said about being off the market for a relationship.

He was definitely off the market for the time being. His entire life had shifted when he'd met his birth mother the first week of May. Until five years ago, he'd never planned on even seeking her out. He'd always believed that his birth mother had given him up to provide him with a better life than she could, for whatever reason, and he'd admired her for that. But his heart and soul were with his parents, the Morrows, who'd adopted him. They'd been great parents, sturdy and steady, and when their surprise baby had come along ten years later, they hadn't loved CJ, their biological son, any differently than they loved Jake.

He knew, without a shadow of a doubt, that he wouldn't feel about his twin brother any more or better or differently than he felt about CJ, who was his brother, period. But Jake felt the call to see the man, to meet him, to know something about this twin brother he'd shared a womb with for nine months. That meant something too; it all meant something, every part of Jake's birth story—from Sarah Mack's pregnancy at sixteen years of age to how Jake felt right now. He had to find his twin and connect with him, even in the slightest way—a letter, an email, hell, even a text. Connection. That's all he wanted. If they met and got to know each other and formed a relationship, even better.

Though, of course, CJ might not think so of that last part. He glanced out the window and could just make out CJ's tall, strong silhouette on Shadow, their black gelding, as he checked on grass levels in a far pasture where they'd be moving the sheep. Yes, CJ was a player and a flirt and hadn't been careful with people's feelings, women's feelings, but Jake wondered if the combination of the death of their parents and Jake's discovery of his biological twin had done a number on the then seventeen-year-old. For the past five years, CJ had broken up with every young woman he dated, from one date to a few months, even if he'd really seemed to like her. Was he leaving them before they could leave him? Hurt him? Break his heart? Maybe.

Jake wasn't sure. CJ had a fun-loving exterior, and it was hard to tell just how deep he truly ran, even if Jake had seen his brother's body shaking with sobs over their parents' deaths, the day it happened and several times after. CJ *felt*; Jake knew that.

Jake stared at his cell phone, sitting on top of a glossy brochure for LoneStar Ranch, a breeding operation in town. *Just call Carson Ford and tell him to get the search for your twin started*, he told himself. It could be just a first step, seeing if the man could be found. But even that seemed a breach of trust. If he was going to look for his twin, he should let CJ know, not start a big inquiry on the down low as though he was sneaking behind his brother's back.

He'd talk to CJ about it tomorrow.

And who knew if Carson Ford would even be able to find his twin? The private investigator had easily found Jake, at his birth mother's request, because he'd left his contact info for his file at the adoption agency. Because, then again, the case had been personal to Carson then and it would be personal this time too. Jake sat back and smiled at the story Carson had finally told him about how he'd come to be involved in looking for him.

Apparently, Carson's father, a widowed banker in Blue Gulch, had gone to a fortune-teller who'd told him that his second great love would be a green-eyed hairstylist named Sarah. Carson had thought his father was nuts for believing in that "malarkey." But his father had believed, and so Carson had gone on the hunt with the fortune-teller's daughter, Olivia Mack, to prove his father wrong—and because Olivia had been sure the mystery woman was her own estranged

aunt. Only thing Carson had done was prove his father
and the fortune-teller right: Sarah Mack and Edmund
Ford had fallen deeply in love. And so had Carson
and Olivia—when neither of them was looking for
love. There was going to be a big double wedding in
the fall, to which Jake was invited and would attend.
And considering that Olivia ran the Hurley's Homestyle Kitchen food truck, where Emma sometimes
helped out, he had no doubt his new cook would be
invited too.

The thought of Emma Hurley brought her pretty
face to mind, her big blue eyes and the long lashes.
He sure wished she was going to the dance.

Would he feel ready for a relationship, for love and
marriage and all that, if he found his twin and settled
that part of his life? Maybe. Then again, he still felt
a bitter sting anytime he thought of his ex, how she'd
bailed on him when he'd wanted to wait, for CJ's sake,
to dig through his past. He'd realized as the days and
months and years had gone by that he'd stopped trust-
ing, stopped expecting anything from anyone.

So, no, this buck would not be asking anyone to
dance tonight. And especially not the only woman he
wanted to dance *with*.

Parking in the center of town at 10:00 a.m. was a
breeze; Emma found a spot right in front of the apricot-colored Victorian that housed Hurley's Homestyle
Kitchen. She loved Blue Gulch. Though the town bor-
dered Oak Creek, where she'd grown up, she hadn't
spent much time with her Blue Gulch relatives. Her father had had some long-ago falling-out with his uncle
and his wife, Essie Hurley, and according to what her

dad had said over the years, he'd tried to tell his uncle and Essie how to run the restaurant, then had gloated when it ran into financially slow patches. The relationship had quickly soured, and Emma had grown up barely knowing Essie or her cousins, who Essie had raised after their parents had died in an accident. But the past weeks that Emma had been in town, living in the Victorian, sneezing up a storm over the puppies despite her allergy medication, had been absolutely wonderful. Emma's dad drove people away with his bossy, controlling way, and right here she had all this family—kind, welcoming, and with a love of cooking in common.

"How's the new boss treating you?" Essie asked, giving Emma a hug in the big country kitchen. Seventy-six-year-old Essie had had a health scare last year, and though she'd cut back on too much time on her feet, her granddaughters had had special chairs made just for her that could reach varying heights, from the worktable to the ovens, to the counters, so she could sit and make her famed sauces and soups and amazing entrées.

"I came downstairs at four thirty this morning to start breakfast, and guess what?" Emma said, tying on her Hurley's Homestyle Kitchen apron. "The whole crew—Hank, Grizzle, Golden and CJ, he's Jake's brother, were all in the kitchen cooking already—everything from eggs to bacon and pancakes with blueberries. They'd felt terrible when they heard I'd come to the ranch looking for Joshua—Tex—only to hear that he'd died in a riding accident. They're a really nice group of cowboys."

"Wait. Grizzle was cooking?" Annabel Hurley

Montgomery asked with a grin. She was dredging chicken wings in flour, and Emma went over to take on the prep.

"You know Grizzle?" Emma asked.

"Sure do," Annabel said. "He used to work at a farm nearby and would come in for lunch every day. When I was thirteen, Georgia and I were picking herbs in the fields out back when we saw that the stray dog that was always hanging around in the river had gotten caught in a current. Georgia and I almost drowned trying to save it and we made so much noise that some people came running. Grizzle jumped right in and saved that dog. But the dog was so scared she bit him. Blood was running down his arms but he held on tight and brought that dog to the riverbank."

"Aww," Emma said, her huge platter of wings ready for the fryer. She grabbed another platter and started on another batch, flour and egg wash under her nails. "Was the dog all right? Was Grizzle all right?"

Annabel nodded. "Both were fine. That dog had taken off the minute its feet hit land, but that night it laid down right on the front porch of Grizzle's house. Grizzle adopted her and named her River. She never bit again. When River was dying and it was time to let her go, Grizzle invited me and my sisters to the little funeral he had in his yard, since we were the ones who brought them together. Remember how we sobbed?" she said to Georgia.

Annabel's older sister, Georgia Hurley Slater, who baked for the restaurant, smiled. "River turned out to be the sweetest dog ever."

Clementine Hurley Grainger, the youngest of her cousins and head waitress, came into the kitchen and said hi to Emma and announced they were having two big groups for lunch, the library's book club, which had close to twenty members, at twelve thirty, and the rancher's association bigwigs at 1:00 p.m. There were only six of them, but they always ordered enough food for double, and Hurley's portions were generous to begin with.

Emma glanced at her cousins, their wedding rings gleaming, and a bit of envy poked at her. The three Hurley sisters had found wonderful husbands, and both Annabel and Georgia had babies. Clementine had a daughter who she'd adopted from foster care and her husband's orphaned twin nephews, and sometimes Emma would see the big family together, wives, husbands, children, and she'd wish she could have that for herself. She had the extended family, sure. But her baby's father was gone. Her mother was long gone. Her own father was, as usual, demanding she live according to his rules for her, so she didn't even have the comfort of her dad in her life right now. She thought of him, missing those rare times when he could be so loving and kind. She sure wished he was by her side right now, but that just couldn't be. She was on her own and would be fine. She had the Hurleys of Blue Gulch, and she'd found a perfect job and place to live. She'd raise her baby among friends, loving friends. *I can do this*, she reminded herself. I *want* to do this.

"Oh, and I ran into Olivia Mack this morning," Clementine added. "She mentioned she'd be coming in for lunch at noon with her husband- and in-laws-to-be."

"Does Olivia need me to cover the food truck this afternoon, then?" Emma asked, dredging what had to be her hundredth chicken wing in flour, then dipping it in the egg wash and coating it in flour again before laying it on the platter. When Emma had first started working at Hurley's, she'd trained at their food truck, which was parked on the other end of Main Street and served po'boys of all kinds and the best cannoli Emma had ever had. Olivia, the cook and manager, had met the man she was marrying this fall while working in the food truck.

"Dylan's working the truck today," Essie said. Dylan, one of their cooks, was just eighteen years old and a single father of an adorable baby boy named Timmy. "I didn't want to overtax you on your first day at the ranch."

Emma smiled at her aunt and got busy. After she had hundreds of chicken wings ready for the fryer for the first wave of the lunch rush, she moved on to assisting Essie, who was working on sauces. Emma loved making barbecue sauce, and Hurley's had at least ten variations. Then she moved on to preparing the spicy coleslaw, which Emma had been craving lately. Forget pickles. Emma could eat smothered pulled pork po'boys with a side of the spicy slaw every day. With a cannoli studded with chocolate chips for dessert. And ice-cold lemonade.

By noon, the restaurant's dining room had filled up. Since there was a line forming, Emma headed out to the entry with a tray of Essie Hurley's famed minibiscuits topped with a bit of apple butter. When Emma had first started working at Hurley's she found they calmed the bit of morning sickness she had. The delicious biscuits also kept hungry customers from getting miffed about the wait time for a table without spoiling their appetites.

"Um, could I... "

At the familiar, tentative voice, Emma turned to see Golden standing in front of her, eyeing the mini-biscuits. But he bit his lip and looked down at his feet. Behind him was Jake, looking incredibly handsome, as usual.

"Would you like a biscuit, Golden? Help yourself," she said, holding the tray a bit closer to him.

He smiled and took one and popped it in his mouth. "Thanks, Emma." Suddenly he started coughing and almost choking, his gaze on someone behind Emma. He moved behind the big faux cactus with the giant red sunglasses, which had been a gift from a competitor to repel business but which customers loved. Golden peered out at the person behind Emma again, then darted behind the cactus. Yeesh. Unless he was hiding from the police or someone who wanted to pummel him, she couldn't imagine what was going on.

Until she followed his sheepish gaze behind her to Katie Walsh, one of the new waitresses. The twenty-three-year-old redhead had been a real find for Hurley's. A part-time student, Katie had studied the menu for her interview and was so knowledgeable about the food and always so nice to everyone that she was quickly making a fortune in tips.

Katie came over with menus and a big smile. "Hi, Jake. Hi there, Golden," she said, peering around the cactus.

Jake smiled. Emma smiled. But Golden turned away and almost knocked over the candy dish of mints and little chocolates and tiny packets of hand wipes.

Katie bit her lip and her face fell. "Table for two?" she asked Jake.

"No, thanks," Jake said. "We're just here for take-out."

Katie directed them toward the short line at the take-out counter where Essie sat taking orders. As Golden slouched out from behind the cactus, practically glued to Jake's back, Katie said, "Going to the dance tonight?"

Golden turned beet red and didn't answer.

"The whole crew will be there," Jake told Katie.

Katie glanced at Golden, but he still didn't turn her way. She looked absolutely crestfallen.

Whoa boy. Golden was definitely going to need a lot of pointers. One night of tips at dinnertime wasn't going to cut it.

"Jake!" someone called from the dining room.

Emma glanced over and saw Sarah Mack, a tall, auburn-haired woman in her late forties, standing and waving at Jake. At Sarah's table was her niece, Olivia Mack, Emma's friend who'd trained her in the food truck, Olivia's fiancé, Carson Ford, a private investigator, and Carson's dad, Edmund Ford. Emma had met Sarah and the Fords a few times while working in the food truck with Olivia, but she didn't know how Jake knew them. He excused himself and walked over. Jake hugged Sarah and there was hand shaking and chitchat.

"Emma!" Olivia called over with a smile. "I can tell you made this amazing grilled po'boy—I always know your delicious sauce."

"And I've snagged her as my new cook," Jake said.

Just then CJ came into the restaurant, but at the sight of Jake talking to Sarah, CJ froze for a moment, then quickly left. Emma wondered what that was about.

As CJ left, Jake's expression completely changed.

"It'll take time for him to get used to the idea," Sarah whispered to Jake.

Okay, Emma was clearly missing something. Who was Sarah Mack to Jake? And what did CJ have to get used to?

Emma realized she was fraternizing instead of working and that she'd better get back into the kitchen.

"See you at home," Jake said, giving her a smile that almost made her forget where she was.

See you at home. Her heart had pinged at those words. What the heck?

It's just nice to hear, she told herself. When she first found out she was pregnant, the idea of someone special waiting for her, someone to come home to at the end of the day, a father for her baby, a life partner was everything she wanted for herself. But the more her baby's father had eluded her, the more she'd realized she truly was on her own and that the only person she could count on was herself. Especially now with Joshua gone, Emma needed to be stronger than she'd ever been. She had a baby to raise—and raise well.

See you at home...

A hand instinctively touched her belly, and she felt tears sting the backs of her eyes. *Lord, woman up*, she yelled at herself. She was supposed to be self-sufficient, not getting all misty-eyed about a man and a home and someone waiting her for.

Danged hormones.

Unsettled, she slipped into the kitchen.

* * *

After her shift at Hurley's Homestyle Kitchen, Emma never wanted to see raw chicken again. But when she'd arrived back at the ranch, she'd overheard Grizzle telling Golden that fried chicken was his lucky food and that anytime he ate fried chicken, good things happened to him. Like when he won a hundred bucks betting on the underdog at the rodeo after buying the three-piece chicken bucket. Or when he took his now-grown daughter to Chicken World during a big argument about something dumb and they'd made up, him getting his way. So Emma made fried chicken for dinner for the crew, with garlic mashed potatoes and green beans, and Grizzle's entire face lit up.

"Oh yeah!" he said when she set down the platter of chicken. "This means something good for the dance tonight."

The dance had been talk of her shift at Hurley's. Everyone was going. Even her seventy-six-year-old aunt with her new beau, who owned the bookstore in town, and her cousins and their families. And the dance was the talk at the dinner table at the Full Circle Ranch.

"So, Golden, you *are* going to the dance, right?" Emma said, handing over the big bowl of mashed potatoes. Part of her felt funny pushing at him, but Jake had asked her to give the cowboys some tips on communicating with the opposite sex, and after witnessing Golden hiding behind a cactus earlier, he was her focus. Hank might offend the women he liked, but at least he could speak to them.

Golden forked a green bean and pushed it around on his plate. "I don't know. I want to. But…"

"Of course you're going," Hank said, slapping him on the back. "Everyone's seen the way you look at Katie."

"And didn't she *ask* you if you were going?" Jake commented after a bite of fried chicken. "That's usually a sign a woman is interested in seeing you there, right, Emma?"

Emma nodded. "Sure is. If she asked, she's hoping she'll see you there. And since it's bucks' choice, she's very likely hoping you'll ask her to dance."

"Can you dance, kid?" Grizzle asked Golden, one eyebrow raised.

"Actually, my older sister taught me. Kind of embarrassing." Red circles appeared on Golden's cheeks and he stared down at his food. "But I don't know. I wouldn't know how to ask or what to say when we're dancing." He shrugged and sat back, and Emma could tell he was really bothered by how his shyness had affected him his whole life.

"I love that your sister taught you," Emma said. "You two must be close. Did you know that Katie has an older sister? She's enlisted right now and Katie misses her a lot. And since you know how to dance, all you have to do is walk right up to Katie and say, 'Would you like to dance with me?'"

"What if she says no?" Golden said.

"Well, then you know you tried," Emma said. "That's all we can do is try, right? Trying is everything. If you don't try, *nothing* happens."

"Unless you're CJ," Grizzle said with a roll of his eyes, "and beauties throw themselves at you."

"Well, CJ has to *try* to avoid getting beat up by

pissed-off exes," Hank said. "I've seen him *try* real hard not to get his pretty-boy face smashed in."

CJ rolled his own eyes. "Emma, this might be the best fried chicken I've ever had. And given that my mom made amazing fried chicken, that's saying something."

Emma smiled at CJ. He might be *trying* very hard right now to change the subject, but that was a very kind thing to say. "Thanks, CJ. That means a lot."

She felt Jake's eyes on her. But when she glanced up, he was looking at his brother. "Mom did make amazing fried chicken, didn't she? God, I miss her."

"Do you?" CJ said so quietly that Emma wasn't even sure she'd heard him right. CJ wasn't looking at Jake; he was pushing around mashed potatoes on his plate.

From the way Jake's expression changed, from sort of wistful to conflicted, she knew she had heard CJ right.

There was dead silence at the table.

"Golden," Emma said, adding some green beans to her plate. "Since Katie asked you if you were going to the dance, I don't think she'll say no to a dance. I think she's counting on you asking."

Golden sat up a little straighter. "Really? You think?"

"I'd bet on it," Emma said.

"Ditto," Jake said.

"We all would," Hank added, a fork stabbed with green beans midway to his mouth. "I'd bet my new truck. And you know how I love that truck."

"Sometimes I think you love that truck more than you love Fern," Grizzle said and burst into laughter.

"Well, the truck doesn't give me guff," Hank muttered.

That got a chuckle from everyone, even CJ, and then talk turned to whether Hank would dare ask Fern to dance, and he said of course he would.

"Not a word about cow manure," Jake said, pointing a finger at his foreman.

Hank rolled his eyes. "I honestly don't see why. Jeez. It's what we *do*."

Emma glanced at Jake and shared a smile with him. Hank might have to keep learning the hard way before it sunk in.

"You're going, right, Emma?" Hank asked.

"Oh, my dancing shoes are put away too," she said, patting her belly.

"You have to go," Hank said. "Golden might need help approaching Katie. And God knows Grizzle will need your guidance."

"Oh, I don't know," Emma said.

"I'll make you a deal," Jake said, his green eyes twinkling devilishly. "Since neither of us plans on dancing, anytime anyone asks you to the dance, you can just say you promised that dance to me, then come find me, and we'll twirl around the floor."

She imagined herself in Jake's arms, being held close, resting her head against him. Part of her wanted that more than anything. But she knew what a dance could lead to. And she wasn't going there. Unless she had to.

She shouldn't skip the dance—not with this bunch needing a charm school for cowboys in real time. "Well, I do work on a ranch now so I should do my part for the rancher's association." She glanced at Jake.

"Thanks for the offer to rescue me. I'll only take you up on it if I absolutely have to."

"Ooh, was that a burn?" Hank asked, looking from Emma to Jake.

"I think it was," Grizzle said, breaking into laughter.

Emma's cheeks had to be bright red. "No! I mean, oh, stop it. I'm just…pregnant."

Jake smiled. "Well, just know if you need me, I'm there."

That was what she was afraid of. Needing.

With empty plates and platters and full bellies, the cowboys got up, again picking up their plates until Emma told them to leave them for her. They headed out, but Jake stopped in the doorway of the dining room.

"Thanks for helping Golden out," he said. "I think he definitely will ask Katie to dance."

"I hope so. It's clear she likes him. I didn't want to say so in case I read it wrong, but it sure looked that way to me."

He nodded and walked over to the sliding glass door, looking out at the land. Something was definitely on his mind. She almost reached out a hand to his shoulder and asked if everything was okay, but he turned around just then and she stepped back. "I need to go talk to my brother. See you later, Emma. And thanks again."

She nodded back. And couldn't help wondering what was going on between the Morrow brothers.

On the second-floor landing, Jake knocked on CJ's bedroom door.

"It's open," his brother called.

Jake went in, a cloud of body spray assailing him from the direction of the bathroom. His brother stood before the rectangular mirror, rubbing gel into his thick, dark hair, still damp from a shower.

"Look, CJ," he began, trying to figure out what to say, how to bring up what CJ had said at dinner regarding Jake's comment about their mother.

God, I miss her.

Do you?

Did CJ really think he'd forgotten their mother, the kind, loving woman who'd raised him, just because he'd found his birth mother and had developed a relationship with her? Apparently so. Or CJ was just rankled by the whole thing.

That afternoon, when CJ had come into Hurley's while Jake had been talking to Sarah Mack, his birth mother, he'd seen the look on CJ's face. And watched him rush back out. CJ had agreed to move to Blue Gulch, which meant he had to be okay with all this on some level. But he'd said he didn't want to talk about Jake's biological family. And he clearly didn't want it in his face.

Hell, maybe CJ wouldn't be ready for Jake to seek out his biological twin brother. Dammit, why was this so complicated? The idea of looking for his twin was fraught enough for Jake—the unknown. The Pandora's box he might he opening. He didn't know who this man was.

He's probably something like you, his birth mother had said last week when they'd been talking about him. Which was one of the reasons he was so comfortable around Sarah Mack. Despite Sarah being on the reserved side, when she did say something, it was always something that made him feel better, untied some knots.

But CJ's feelings mattered. They mattered a whole hell of a lot.

Jake headed over to the wall of windows in the large room and looked out at the front yard, at land that stretched as far as he could see. He knew CJ loved the Full Circle, loved the hundreds of acres of land and the big, majestic farmhouse. Moving away from home had been good for both of them, and he knew his brother had given up some sense of comfort by agreeing to move to Blue Gulch. He'd done that for Jake.

"I do miss Mom. Mom and Dad. I miss them all the time," Jake said. He'd been grief-stricken when their wonderful parents had been killed in a car accident. And he'd taken his responsibility to his brother, just seventeen then, very seriously. For a long time it had been just the two of them, the Morrow brothers. Then a notation scrawled on his adoption document had changed everything.

Yes, Jake understood how his brother felt—about all of it.

CJ glanced at Jake as he came out of the bathroom and headed toward his closet. He spent a good few minutes going through his shirts, finally choosing a dark green chambray button-down and then easing a brown leather belt through the loops of his dark jeans.

"It's just… I don't really want to talk about it," CJ said, turning away.

"CJ," Jake began. But he didn't know what to say, exactly. What he wanted CJ to know was that he'd never stop being his brother. Never stop being there for him. No matter what. A twin wouldn't ever change things between them. But bringing all that up right now, before a dance, seemed the wrong time and place. CJ seemed a bit broody as it was over whatever was going on with the woman he liked. Stella.

"Forget it, Jake," CJ said. "Everything's fine. The fried chicken reminded me of Mom and I said something. That's all."

But he knew that wasn't all.

"Go get ready for the dance," CJ said. "I'm fine."

Meaning: *stop looking at me with that older brother expression. We're done here.*

Jake moved over where CJ stood at his dresser, rummaging through his socks. He put a hand on CJ's shoulder and nodded, then headed to the door.

Jake didn't want to talk about any of this, either. But they had to.

"By the way, your plan's gonna backfire on you," CJ said as Jake was leaving. "Emma will be hounded by dance partners. You'll be dancing *every* dance with her."

"Fine by me," Jake said—without thinking.

His brother's eyes lit up. "Ah, that's how it is. You *like* her."

Jake frowned. "I just—" He cleared his throat. "She's pregnant and on her own and I'm her boss. That's all."

CJ laughed. "Right." He laughed again and Jake shot him a glare as he continued down the hall.

He *did* like her. *Too* much.

Chapter Four

The kitchen clean from dinner, Emma sat on the patio with Redford beside her, watching a squirrel in the yard. It had been a long day, a good day, and she was tired and ready for a long soak in a bubble bath, but it seemed she had a cowboy's hair and beard to tame and a dance to attend. She headed back inside just as Jake was coming down the stairs.

His conversation with CJ hadn't gone well—that she could tell just by Jake's expression. He seemed preoccupied, his shoulders tense, his jaw hard.

"Everything okay?" she asked.

He nodded. "Family stuff."

"I know how that is," she said, her father's disapproving face floating into her mind.

He kept his gaze on her as he came down the stairs. "Your dad?"

"He wants me to move back home so he can raise my child right—and his way. He has a list of suitable husband candidates he wants me to meet before I— and I quote—'lose my figure.' He didn't like his culinary school trained daughter working in a diner and he certainly won't like it that I'm a cook for cowboys on a ranch in Blue Gulch."

"Sorry," Jake said. "I'm sure that right now you could use his emotional support."

"That's exactly right. It's all I want. To know my father is there for me, that he loves me and cares about me. The conflict between us just makes me feel more alone than ever."

He reached for her hand and held it for a moment, and the strong warmth of it was like a soothing balm. "I'm glad you're going to the dance, then. Maybe it'll take your mind off things. You'll listen to some music, sway a bit, drink some weak punch."

She smiled, then glanced at the grandfather clock against the wall. "I'd better get to the bunkhouse barn." She pulled the comb from her bag and held it up. "This comb and I have a date with Grizzle."

He grinned, and she was glad to see the worry and strain gone from his expression. But as she was leaving, she turned and both were back on his handsome face. Part of her wanted to stay and talk, but she'd promised Grizzle she'd show up an hour before the dance, and it was now just minutes to seven o'clock.

Emma walked the quarter mile to the other big red barn. The arched white door was closed but there was no bell so Emma knocked. Silence. She knocked again. Nothing. She tried the handle and the door opened.

Huh. Not what she was expecting. She didn't know

what she was expecting, really; she'd assumed the crew didn't sleep in actual bunks in a barn with hay on the floor. But this building was really more like an apartment building just in the shape of a barn. There was an entry way with coatracks and boots storage, then four doors, labeled Bunk 1 and so on with each crew's name on an engraved plaque magnet.

Number two was Grizzle's door. She knocked.

"Open!" he called back.

She opened the door to find a small living room with a rug, a plush beige couch and a big screen TV. Grizzle came out of a back doorway; she could see a bed and a dresser. So the barn was really like a small apartment building.

"I made the mistake of looking in the mirror after my shower," Grizzle said with a frown, his thick wiry hair poking up in every direction. "Maybe I should just forget this whole thing."

"After I went to all the trouble of getting you this?" she asked, pulling out the comb she'd bought for a buck at the drugstore. "I also bought a little hair gel. I promise to just use a bit."

"Let's get this over with," he said.

The only mirror in the entire apartment was in the bathroom, so they headed in there, but it turned out Grizzle didn't want to see until she was done, or maybe not at all, so she had him sit down at the small square table by the window.

"Uh-oh," Grizzle said. "There goes Goatby again." He upped his chin out the window, and there was Jake and CJ chasing after the black goat up the field.

Emma's heart skipped a beat at the sight of Jake. He must have caught sight of the goat's escape while getting dressed because he was shirtless, wearing only dark jeans that looked brand-new and nice brown leather cowboy boots.

She almost dropped the comb. My God, he was a thing to behold. His chest and arms were so muscular.

"He's available," Grizzle said. "But not really."

"What? I'm not—" Emma said, feeling her cheeks burn. "But what do you mean 'not really'?"

"Oh, he got burned bad by his last girlfriend. And what with all the family stuff, well, he's just all tied up in knots."

"Family stuff?" she repeated. There it was again.

"Oh, I shouldn't be talking about the boss behind his back," Grizzle said, then clammed up.

Emma glanced out the window and bit her lip. She wondered what was going on. She couldn't take her eyes off Jake as she headed back toward the big barn with Goatby on a lead.

He's available, but not really. Well, that was good, wasn't it? She was available but not really. She knew what that meant. She was single, but she wasn't looking for a relationship. She was her own woman and would make her own way. She didn't need rescuing, no matter what her father thought or said.

And clearly, Jake was the same. But she didn't like the thought of Jake Morrow being tied up in knots. He was a good man, clearly, cared about his brother and the men who worked for him at the Full Circle. He deserved all the happiness in the world. Maybe she could apply some of her "tips for unruly cowboys" to him.

"Well, let's see," she said to Grizzle, assessing him. She eyed the wild gray-brown wiry hair, going in every which way, down to the end of his neck. She reached for her spray bottle and gave his hair a spritz, then worked in a bit of gel, which had a nice, clean masculine scent.

"I feel stupid," Grizzle said, frowning. "Are you done yet?"

She laughed. "Couple minutes and you'll be free."

She worked the gel through, then combed his hair, giving him an unstructured side part that wouldn't look too "done." She ran her fingers through the mass to make sure his hair wouldn't dry sticky or crunchy. "Okay, we'll wait for that to dry. Now for the beard."

He rolled his eyes and she had to laugh.

She used the spray bottle again and a tiny bit of gel to just tame the beard as much as she could, and what a difference both made. The beard was still mountain man, but looked groomed instead of a messy wild thatch.

She stepped back and almost gasped. "Wow, Grizzle. With your hair and beard groomed some, those beautiful blue eyes of yours really stand out."

"I might as well see what you did to me," he grumbled.

He walked into the bathroom and she heard him gasp. "I look…ten years younger!"

She laughed. "You sure do."

"Huh. Think I should put on a different shirt?" he asked.

"You were planning to wear that?" she asked, chuckling. He was wearing one of his work shirts, gray chambray with his name and the ranch embroidered on the side. She could see a mustard stain, which had to be from lunch, and the shirt kind of smelled like blue cheese from the salad at dinner.

"Maybe a nice plaid shirt, button-down with crisp jeans?"

"Crisp?" he repeated, titling his head.

"You know, dark wash and fresh from the dryer?"

"I have lots of faded jeans and a pair of black pants. I do have one pair of those khaki things. Should I wear those?"

Emma smiled. "Those sound just right. And those brown boots by the door instead of your work boots."

Fifteen minutes later, when Grizzle was all ready, Emma couldn't believe her eyes. The man had been transformed.

Grizzle was tall enough but seemed to stand even taller now that he was so presentable. "So you think if I asked someone to dance, she'd be happy about it instead of disappointed that she had to?"

"Absolutely," Emma said.

He lifted his chin. "Huh. I guess we'll see."

"I'd better go get ready myself," she said. "See you there."

"See you there. Oh, and, Emma?"

She turned around by the door. "Thanks."

"You're very welcome," she said, her heart bursting for the man.

"You'd better wear a burlap sack," Grizzle said as she was leaving. "And sneakers. Your feet will be killing you after having to dance every dance. You're the new gal."

"Oh, I'm not worried about that. I've ensured that no one will ask me to dance."

"How'd you do that?" he asked.

She smiled at the thought of the little gift she'd bought herself in town last week. It would be perfect for tonight. "You'll see."

* * *

"Um, Emma?" Jake heard CJ say just outside his home office. "No offense but…"

"But what?" Emma asked.

Okay, what was this about? Jake could hear CJ and Emma talking in the hallway by the bottom of the stairs. He came out of his office to find his brother looking at Emma as if she had four heads and Emma smiling proudly.

"Emma, trust someone who knows a thing or two about guys and relationships," CJ said. "No one— and I mean *no one*—is going to ask you to dance if you wear that."

"That's exactly why I'm wearing it," Emma said, glancing down at her shirt.

Jake smiled at Emma's silky yellow tank top with Baby On Board in rhinestones across the front. A rhinestone arrow pointed down to her belly. She wore a denim skirt and silver sandals and looked absolutely beautiful.

"If it's rude to say no at a bucks' choice dance," she added, "I thought I'd let my condition do the talking for me."

"I know you said you were off the market, but don't you *want* a father for your baby?" CJ asked.

Jake frowned at him. *A little personal, CJ.* Still, he was glad CJ had no manners and had asked. Jake wanted to know.

"I can support my baby on my own," she said. "I have a job, a nice place to live, and Jake already said it won't be any problem for me to bring the little one to work when he or she comes along. A bassinet, a playpen, and I can take care of him or her just fine while I'm in the kitchen.

"Oh, I didn't necessarily mean financially," CJ said. "I meant—" His phone pinged with a text. He pulled his cell from his pocket and looked at it, his face falling. "Oh hell. Now Stella says she might not be going to the dance. She says she can't believe anything I say. Do you believe *that*?" He frowned.

It took everything in Jake not to say "yes, *I do* believe that."

CJ's scowled deepened. "Well, if she goes, I'll just make her jealous and then she'll realize how much she wants me."

"Um, CJ," Emma said. "If she's already nervous about your reputation as a serial dater, I don't think making her jealous at the dance is the way to approach winning her heart."

"Emma, with all due respect, I have *a lot* of experience with women." He smiled and rolled his eyes in an exaggerated way and headed toward the door. "See you there," he said with a grin as though he had nothing to worry about.

Jake shook his head. "He's going to learn the hard way too."

"Yup," Emma said.

"Grizzle let you near him with that comb?" he asked.

"He did! Wait till you see him. You might not recognize him."

"Shall we go?" he asked, offering his arm.

"Oh," she said, taking a step back. "I didn't realize we were going together."

He dropped his arm. "Well, not together, together.

Of course. But we are going to the same place, so I'm happy to drive."

"Right," she said. "Sorry. That would be great."

He didn't offer his arm again, but he wanted to.

To a woman with a Baby on Board tank top.

In the first half hour, Emma had been asked to dance three times.

"You might have a baby on board but I don't see a ring," a tall, skinny man in a black Stetson said, holding out his hand as a country song blared from the band on the stage.

Despite the man's warm smile, Emma gulped as she had the past two times. The song was a slow ballad. "Thanks for asking. But I promised every dance to someone."

Which was how she'd ended up in Jake's arms for the third time.

He smelled like soap and the slightest hint of a spicy aftershave. "Back again," he said with a laugh.

"Sorry," she said. What if he didn't want to dance with her? Then again, he was the one who'd come up with the idea. Just being nice. And now he was stuck with her.

Except there was something about the way he was holding her that felt so...comfortable. So comforting. He wasn't holding her like a man who had to. But like a man who *wanted* to.

"I'm sorry that CJ got so nosy," he said. "I think he's trying to work out some things for himself so he's full of questions."

"I don't mind at all," she said. "I'm glad it's out in

the open—that I'm not looking for a husband. I can stand on my own two feet."

He held her gaze and nodded. "Well, just know if you ever need anything, to say the word."

This felt too good. The way he held her, the way she was able to forget everything and just move to the music and the singer's melodic voice. Part of her wanted to pull away but most of her was staying put.

"You sure country dance good for an Oak Creek girl," Hank said from behind her.

Emma raised an eyebrow at the foreman, who was standing close by with a bottle of beer. He looked great—a nicely pressed Western-style shirt and dark jeans and unscuffed cowboy boots. His thick red hair looked freshly cut. "Hank, that sounds as though you're saying Oak Creek women are too snooty to enjoy country-Western dances at a rancher's association fund-raiser."

Hank looked confused. "But that *is* what I'm saying."

Jake shook his head. "You can see how a woman from Oak Creek might take offense, Hank."

Hank shrugged. "Take offense at the truth? I don't get it."

Hank's rough edges sure weren't going to be easy to smooth over, Emma thought. "Hank, did you ask Fern to dance?"

"The minute I approached her, without saying a single word, she said 'No, Hank' and turned away." The foreman scowled.

"Well, how about this," Emma said. "What if you try again and very politely tell her she looks lovely this evening and would she like to dance. See how that goes."

Hank all but snorted. "*Lovely?* I don't talk like that."

"Try 'nice,' then," Jake suggested.

"Oh fine," Hank said, rolling his eyes. "If that's what I have to do."

Jake laughed as Hank squared his shoulders and marched up to Fern.

Emma could see Fern lift her chin and listen. And then all of a sudden, she was following Hank on the dance floor.

Success!

"Well, well," Jake said. "We make a good team."

She smiled. A team. The word filled her with warmth and chilled her at the same time. "Oh no," she said, upping her chin to the left. "I see Golden. He's just sitting at the table in the back, slouched down." She glanced around. "And there's Katie, on the dance floor with some other guy."

"Let's go rescue him," Jake said. "Give him some courage."

She smiled and they headed over. A team. "Hey, Golden. Song will be changing soon. Katie's right there." She pointed at where she stood dancing with a guy Emma recognized as a Hurley's regular.

Golden looked terrified. "I can't. I just can't. I don't even know what to say."

"You just say, 'Katie, would you like to dance?'"

Jake nodded. "That's it."

Golden squeezed his eyes shut and looked like he might throw up. When the song ended and Katie began walking away from the dance area, Golden looked at

Jake and Emma, then sucked in a breath and got up and started walking toward her.

"Oh, hi, Golden! Having a good time?" Katie asked.

Emma watched the poor guy freeze. His mouth started moving and then he just hurried away. Katie's fell face. But in two seconds, Dylan, the cook at Hurley's, had her twirling to a pop song.

"Poor guy," Emma said. "He may take more time to help out in the romance department than all the others combined."

Jake watched Golden drop back down on the bench. "Well, if he wants to make sure Katie doesn't get away, he'll get there. Sometimes, a person needs a meaningful enough goal."

She nodded. "Just look at Hank. He and Fern are still dancing!"

"You know, Hank's delivery might not be on the money but the sentiment is there— You *are* a good dancer."

"Well, I might be from fancy Oak Creek but I grew up on a farm. It was passed down from four generations of my mother's family. Some light dairy production but mostly produce, particularly apples. I went to quite a few Rancher Association dances in my teen years." The thought of the farm filled her with such a sudden pang of sadness that she had to go sit down.

"Emma?" Jake said, following her over. "You okay?"

It had to be the hormones. What was with all these sudden yearnings for home?

Jake sat down beside her and his nearness added to her confusion. How could she want to be on her own and want him so danged equally? Maybe it was just lust.

Except Emma wanted more than just to rip off Jake Morrow's clothes and see all those glorious muscles.

"I guess I'm not always okay about how things are," she said, hating how weak she sounded to her own ears. "When I graduated from high school, I was there, at home, and working the farm, but my father was horrified," she said. "He kept saying we had a staff to run the farm and that I needed to concentrate on going to college and finding a solid family to marry into. Eventually it drove me away. I moved out, got an apartment on Main Street in Oak Creek and went to culinary school, but the fancy restaurants I worked in after didn't suit me. When I started working at the diner, my father was embarrassed for both of us. He's even more horrified now that I'm pregnant and on my own."

"But you're doing fine."

"He doesn't see it that way. My father is very traditional and proper and cares very much what people think. A daughter having a baby out of wedlock is embarrassing to him."

"I'm sorry there's so much conflict between you," Jake said and his green eyes were so full of compassion that she wanted to just throw herself into his arms and be held. For just a minute. "That must be rough."

Emma was about to respond when she noticed Fern pouring her beer over Hank's head. The folks around them were half laughing and half shocked. "Oh no! Hank must have come out with a real doozy."

Jake looked over, cringing for his foreman, who was sopping wet and headed for the restroom. "Well,

Hank's in trouble, as usual, and Golden is still sitting on the sidelines, but Grizzle's on the floor with Michelle—she's the librarian in Blue Gulch."

In her heels, Michelle was almost as tall as Grizzle. And he sure looked like he was having fun. He caught her eye and winked at her, and Emma laughed. It was so wonderful to have her mind taken off her father and the family farm. "Now, we just have to see how CJ is doing with Stella. I don't see him anywhere, do you?" she said, looking around.

But suddenly, Emma froze, every muscle tensing.

"Emma? What's wrong?" Jake asked.

"I see my father." *Please be a look-alike*, she thought. But it wasn't. "Oh my God, that's my dad. He's standing by the door, looking around. And he does not look like he's here to dance."

Because she was staring at him, Reginald Hurley looked over and their gazes locked. She saw him glaring at her shirt, disgust etching into his expression. He crossed the room toward her.

"Dad?" Emma said. "I'm surprised to see you here. You haven't come to a Rancher Association dance in years."

"I'm not here to dance, Emma," Reginald snapped. "I made a decision today and wanted to talk to you immediately. I went to Hurley's to find you and heard you work at a ranch now but a waitress said that everyone in town is probably at the dance. I thought, well of course Emma won't be at the dance—she's pregnant. So I went to the ranch and no one was there. And here you are, actually advertising that you're pregnant out of wedlock. Thank God this isn't Oak Creek."

Emma was half angry, half shocked. "Dad. I'm a grown woman! And this is the twenty-first century!"

"There's something called propriety no matter what year it is, Emma Leigh Hurley. I have two colleagues who are very interested in meeting you and taking on the baby as their own. I'll send them out to the Full Circle tomorrow. I don't know if you work Sundays, but I chose off times in the event you do. Expect one husband candidate at two and the other at three. Both are very good men, come from good families. You could have a June wedding. Wouldn't that be nice?"

Emma stared at her father, her mouth hanging open. He had to be kidding. She could see he wasn't. Didn't he hear how he sounded? How crazy? "Dad, you cannot be serious."

Reginald Hurley stared back. "Oh, I'm as serious as a heart attack."

Emma lifted her chin. "I will *not* interview husband-father candidates—particularly ones chosen for me. I'm perfectly capable of standing on my own two feet and raising my child."

"The same old story, Emma," Reginald said, his eyes cold. "If you do not choose a suitable man to marry, I'm selling the farm. Your mother would turn over in her grave at your situation and you know it."

Emma froze, then panic overtook her. "You can't sell the farm. Dad, you love that farm. I love that farm. It was in Mom's family for generations." *And one day it's going to be my baby's.*

"I can do whatever I want," he said. "Isn't that your motto? Doing whatever the hell you want? Emma, marriage is a partnership between two people who can give each other a good life. It's not about making out at a rodeo because you think some cowboy is handsome. That's how you ended up alone and pregnant. Marriage, especially with a baby on the way, is about making the right choice and setting up a good life. If you're unwilling to do that, I see no reason to keep the farm in the family. Tradition means nothing to you."

Jake took a step forward. "Mr. Hurley, with all due respect." He extended his hand. "I'm Jake Morrow. I own the Full Circle, where Emma is now the cook and—"

"Look, Morrow, I drove out to your ranch just ten minutes ago. It's a nice operation, granted. But Emma doesn't belong there. I appreciate that you took her in and gave her a job. But enough is enough." He turned to Emma. "Two o'clock and three o'clock for your interviews, Emma."

With that he turned and walked out. Emma opened her mouth to call him back, to plead with him, but he pushed through the door.

And no one "took me in," she wanted to yell from the rooftops. *I got myself a job. I got myself a place to live. I'm taking care of myself and my own.*

Emma dropped back down in the chair, trying to process everything that had just happened. Oh God. Her father's words echoed in her head. "He's going to sell my mother's farm unless I marry one of his colleagues? This can't be happening."

"He'll see reason, Emma," Jake said. "He's bluffing."

"I don't know. He's *very* conservative and traditional. But I'm not marrying a man I don't love. And I'm not planning on loving anyone, so there will be no marrying at all."

Jake squeezed her hand. "He won't make good on his threat. He can't. Come on."

"I have no doubt he will, actually," Emma said. "To Reginald, he's doing the right thing, what must be done."

"Sending strangers for you to interview?" Jake asked, his expression incredulous. "Strangers who want to help raise your child? What?"

Emma's legs suddenly felt like rubber. She was surprised she was already sitting down. Her shoulders slumped. "He'll do just that. And if I don't do as he says, he'll sell my mother's family home. That farm means the world to me."

"I guess your dad knows your currency." Jake shook his head. "What a mess."

"What the hell am I going to do?" she asked.

Chapter Five

As Jake drove Emma home from the dance, he almost pulled over because a crazy thought flashed through his mind.

I'll marry you so you can keep the farm. Given how Emma's father had talked about the Full Circle Ranch, the man would probably think Jake fit under Suitable Husbands for My Daughter, even if he was a rancher and didn't work in an office building.

But even though Jake might not be interested in marriage or love right now, marriage was forever to him. Love meant something. He couldn't offer to marry Emma just to save her farm.

Besides, Emma had made it crystal clear she wasn't interested in marrying anyone. She was determined to stand on her own two feet.

Of course, when she met one of the suits tomorrow

night, it might be love at first sight and maybe she'd change her mind about love and marriage. Unlikely, but still. You never knew.

He scowled. He didn't want that to happen, though. Yeah, he wanted Emma to be happy, and of course he wanted her to have love and happily-ever-after. Which meant he should support her meeting these two Suits tomorrow and encourage her to go with her feelings.

Emma wasn't going to fall in love with one of the Suits. He had no doubt. But she might choose to marry one to save the farm.

Which brought him back to *like hell*.

Maybe when the Suits drove up he could tell them they had the wrong ranch. Or that Emma was experiencing terrible morning sickness and they'd have to come back…never.

Oh hell.

As Jake turned his SUV at the sign for the Full Circle, Emma finally spoke since leaving the dance. "Okay, I've formed a plan. I'll just stall for time until I can figure out how to make my father understand. Yes. That's what I'll do."

Jake glanced at her. She looked equally weary and determined. "How will you stall? You have two candidates coming to the door tomorrow afternoon."

"I'll interview them to show my father I'm at least willing to see things his way and then report that neither was acceptable for this or that reason. He'll have to come up with others. Between those times, I'll talk to him, try to get him to see reason. He can't sell the farm."

"Sounds like a good plan to me," Jake said. He could just see her father scowl at the news that she found neither candidate acceptable and Reginald Hurley sending two more the next day. And the next day. And the next day.

The Full Circle was not going to be overrun by Suits trying to marry his Emma.

What? *His* Emma? Where the hell had that come from?

He was so discombobulated by the notion that he changed the subject. "The farm sure means a lot to you, huh."

She nodded and then seemed lost in thought. "It's where I grew up. It's where I had all my firsts. And it's where all my memories of my mother are."

Memories, Jake thought, uneasiness hitting him in the stomach. "I can understand that." His mother's kind face and warm hazel eyes floated into his mind. Her big breakfasts on weekend mornings. Hugs and Band-Aids for bad bicycle wipeouts. Someone he could always talk to. A loving anchor. "Sometimes I wonder if it was wrong of me to ask CJ to leave Mill Valley—that's where we lived before we moved here just a month ago. We lost our parents five years ago. CJ was only seventeen. All his memories are there." He shook his head. "God, I was selfish. I wanted to move to Blue Gulch because my birth mother is here and I wanted to get to know her. I took CJ away from everything, all his memories."

"But surely CJ wouldn't have joined you here if he didn't want to. He's twenty-two. A grown man."

"I know you're right. And really, all that was left in Mill Valley was a bitter uncle who was constantly suing us over the right to the ranch. He and CJ once even got into a fistfight. The good memories got kind of trampled on until the place just became a hotbed of anger."

"Sounds like a fresh start was the right thing, then," Emma said.

"Except the fresh start involved my birth mother—and the idea that I have a biological twin brother out there somewhere."

Emma gasped. "A twin brother."

He told her about finding the paperwork and the notation and meeting Sarah Mack. He gave her the one-minute version of his life story, including the part about the almost fiancée ditching him when he'd initially dropped the idea of finding his birth mother.

"Ah, now a few things make sense that hadn't before," she said. "Wow. That *is* complicated. I guess we both have some big family issues pressing on us right now."

"You do have a good plan, Emma," he reminded her. "It's solid. It might be just a stall tactic, but like you said, stalling is what you need in order to let your dad calm down some and see reason. Then you'll be able to talk to him. Lay down your *own* plans."

She bit her lip. "It's my hope. But at the same time, I know my dad. He's tough."

He squeezed her hand, wishing he could do more for her. She had enough going on right now without this ultimatum thrown at her.

As the ranch house came into view, Jake's head was about to explode. *CJ. Emma and her husband candidates.*

CJ and his twin.

He pulled up in the parking area and got out to open Emma's door, but she'd hopped out already. As they were heading in, CJ's little sports car came barreling down the drive.

His brother didn't look happy as he got out and stomped toward the front door. He nodded at Jake and then turned to Emma. "Forget what I said about my knowing a thing about relationships. I don't understand women at all. Obviously." He scowled.

"What's going on?" Jake asked.

The moonlight cast a glow over his brother's handsome face, and Jake was struck by just how young he looked. Twenty-two was both old enough and very young at the same time.

"Stella showed up at the dance—of course when I was dancing with another woman. I'd waited a half hour for her before I asked anyone! So Stella sees me and I see her turn around to leave. So I run up to her and she says if I want to date her again it's either exclusive or no deal. Can you believe that?"

"Well, yes, I can, CJ," Jake said. "You've gone out with Stella how many times?"

CJ thought about that. "Eight or nine. Maybe ten."

Jake smiled. "So you clearly have feelings for her."

"Yes, but that doesn't mean I'm ready to stop seeing other people," CJ said.

"*Are* you seeing other women?" Emma asked.

"Well, no. But I like to reserve the right," CJ said.

Emma nodded. "I see the issue here. But it means you can't date Stella."

CJ frowned. "Right, but that's not fair. I'm not ready for a commitment."

"I guess you'll need to think about how much you really do like her," Jake said. "If she's worth giving up other women for."

"She said she wasn't even sure she could count on me even if I *did* commit," CJ said. "Like anyone can count on anybody. Life is a damned crapshoot."

Ah. Jake had a feeling that CJ's issues with dating every woman in Texas and now not being able to commit to a woman he clearly cared a lot about had something to do with what was going on lately. Going on for the past five years, maybe. His brother had lost a lot—young. And for the past five years he'd felt threatened by Jake's birth family, out there, this abstract but very real constant worry that he'd lose his older brother—the person who'd always been there for him.

"Stuff happens, yes," Jake said. "But you *can* count on people. Having faith in the people around you— even strangers, sometimes—is everything."

"Right. Emma had faith in Tex and look what—" CJ stopped, seeming to realize he should.

Emma's face fell, and Jake stepped forward, ready to throttle his brother. But he knew CJ was coming from a place of hurt and insecurity.

"CJ, that was uncalled for," Jake said.

Emma touched Jake on the arm and turned to CJ. "Sometimes the faith you need is in yourself, CJ."

CJ scowled and opened the front door. "I have faith in myself. I know I can only count on myself."

"And me," Jake pointed out. "And the crew."

CJ headed inside, Jake and Emma behind him. He walked to the stairs, then turned, his expression conflicted. "You're a great older brother. And, hell yeah, I appreciate everything you've done for me. But you've got your own thing going."

"CJ, I—"

"It's late," CJ said. "I'm going to bed."

With that, he stomped upstairs.

Jake closed the front door, letting out a breath. "Sometimes CJ can be his own worst enemy."

"Can't we all," Emma said with a sigh. "Is 'your own thing going' your birth family?" Emma asked.

Jake nodded. "I know it troubles him. Five years ago he wasn't ready for me to track down even my birth mother. And I think he's made peace that I have. But the brother thing—that's really affecting him. And CJ comes first to me."

"But you really want to find your twin?"

He nodded and walked to the window, looking out at the inky sky. "It's all I can think about sometimes. The curiosity burns me up."

"I can understand that," she said, putting a hand on his shoulder.

He turned suddenly and kissed her, both soft and hard at the same time, and she responded, wrapping her arms around his neck and drawing him even closer. He'd done it without thinking. She felt so good in his arms, her lips so sweet.

"I can't," she said, pulling away. "I can't. I don't know—I'm..."

He leaned back against the window. "It's okay, Emma. The moment got us. That's all."

But it was a moment he wished could have gone on for hours. Just the brush of her lips on his had set every nerve ending on fire. Everything in him responded to her so close against him. He'd thought he'd been in sweet torment while they'd been dancing a few times earlier tonight? Ha. Nothing compared to the feel of her pressed to him just now, her mouth on his, her soft, cool hands on his neck. Had he ever wanted a woman so bad?

"The moment. Yes. Well, I'd better head up. Thanks for saving me from the dances."

He dragged his gaze off her. Be casual, man, he told himself. "Anytime."

What troubled him, as he walked away, was that he meant it.

Emma was off Sundays and it was nice to sleep in a bit. When she came downstairs for breakfast at seven, she could see only Jake and Grizzle in the dining room, a platter of scrambled eggs and bacon and bagels on the table.

She was craving bacon like crazy.

She was craving Jake like crazy too. She couldn't take her eyes off him. He was reading the local news on an iPad and sipping coffee, his dark green shirt making his eyes even greener. She couldn't stop replaying the kiss.

Which wouldn't happen again. Couldn't happen again. Didn't Emma know what happened when she gave in to her feelings? When she let go? She had a baby at stake. A baby who needed her mother's head screwed on straight.

She took a deep breath, suddenly wondering if her father had the right idea. An arranged marriage. No love, but a fondness, perhaps, an appreciation of the other. A true partnership where each provided prediscussed and settled-on contributions to the marriage. A father figure for her baby who'd be there, steady and sturdy. An arrangement.

What happened to standing on her own two feet?

Your baby needs a father. Stop being so selfish.

Those were some of her father's shots at her over the past month. Some women had babies on their own by choice. Emma didn't think those women were selfish. Some women were left by their baby's father.

Maybe it didn't matter what Emma thought about any of it. If she didn't marry a "suitable man," her father would sell her mother's beloved farm. Her baby's legacy. That couldn't happen.

"Well, look who it is," Grizzle said as she entered the dining room. "The young lady who made me presentable enough for six dances with Michelle and a date with her on Wednesday."

Emma smiled. Grizzle's hair was back to its usual ways. "That's great! Congratulations!" Phew, she was relieved. If Grizzle had gone through all that transforming for nothing, he would be harder to convince to try again.

"Turns out there's more to Michelle than her height," Grizzle added. "Did you know she's read forty-seven books this year? She keeps a list. I know she's a librarian, but still. She reads about two a week. Two a week!"

"And here I am, reading the news digitally," Jake said, taking a sip of his coffee. "Morning, Emma."

She could feel Jake watching her. From his expression she knew he was thinking about last night. Her father. The ultimatum. The unexpected kiss.

Not to mention CJ. Jake Morrow had a whole lot going on in his own life and here she was, a couple days on the job and complicating it further.

She'd meet candidate number one at two o'clock and the next guy at three and, as she'd decided last night, she'd simply stall a bit until she could figure out how to reach her father, make him see reason. As long as she kept reminding herself of that, the panic abated a bit. For two minutes. Then she'd think about the ultimatum her father had dropped on her, and the panic came rushing back. Along with a stabbing hurt.

"Well, gotta run," Grizzle said, taking a piece of bacon to go. "Golden promised to teach me how to text today."

Jake smiled. "Didn't your daughter try last time she visited?"

"Well, I've got to keep up with technology if I'm going to be dating. Plus Michelle said she'd text me with a book recommendation and I don't want to miss it," he said before hurrying out.

Aww. Grizzle's excitement was enough to pull Emma out of her worries. She laughed. "I love seeing Grizzle happy. Who knew a comb could work such magic?"

"It's nice to see you smiling too," Jake said. "I know you couldn't have slept much."

"I didn't." She went into the kitchen to make herself a cup of herbal tea, then came back into the dining room and sat across from Jake. "I still can't believe my father is serious about sending these strangers over, but I know he is."

"So how are you going to run these husband candidate interviews, anyway?" Jake asked. "Will you come up with a list of questions?"

Emma served herself some scrambled eggs and a slice of whole wheat toast. "A list? I don't care what either man has to say about anything!"

Jake took another sip of coffee. "Yes, but perhaps if

you had a list of questions and neither man answered them to your satisfaction, you'd have something tangible to tell your dad about why neither was right for you while you worked on the stalling."

Evil genius! "That's brilliant," she said. "Will you help me come up with questions?"

Jake stood and went into the kitchen and returned with a pencil and a legal pad of yellow paper. "Question one—'How many diapers have you changed in your lifetime? What? *None?*' You'll just jot down *that* unsuitable answer. 'Are you willing to attend a baby care class every night after work for two weeks and on Saturdays? Why yes, Candidate, of course I'm serious. You will be caring for the baby as an equal partner, won't you? Won't you?'"

As Jake's evil grin spread and he broke into laughter, Emma's own smile faded.

He put down the pen. "What's wrong? Did I go too far?"

"Well, it's just that I figured I'd be raising my child myself."

"I know, but for the purposes of the interviews, well, that's what a partner is for, Emma. To help you. To change diapers. To take care of the little one if you're sick. To be there one hundred percent."

"Would be nice to count on someone," Emma said. "But—"

But like CJ had said last night, you could only count on yourself.

Suddenly, Emma's head wasn't screwed on as straight as she thought. You had to count on people. You had to have faith in others. Or you'd be miserable. But here she was, acting like she was a lone wolf.

Now she was back to wondering if an arranged marriage *wasn't* such a terrible plan.

"You know what I want answered most of all?" Emma said. "How you know which is the right way to go. Sometimes, one way seems right. But then the other route does too. How do you know you're making the right choice?"

"I think about that all the time," he said. "Especially when it comes to CJ and looking for my twin," he added on a whisper. "I haven't asked Carson Ford— he's the private investigator who first called me on behalf of my birth mother—to start the search because I don't know if it's the right choice. Right now, I've got to think about CJ. So I find myself holding off. That's allowing your gut to choose. And I think that sometimes, that's the only way you can go."

She nodded and sipped her tea, the hot chamomile instantly soothing. What did her gut say right now? To count on herself.

But if she ignored her father's ultimatum, she'd lose her mother's farm.

"What if someone else holds the cards, though?" she said.

"Like your dad?" he asked.

She nodded. She'd lost her appetite for the bacon she'd been craving a minute ago.

"I think the same rule applies. Go with your gut. Right now it's telling you to go along with his plans to stall him. So do that. Interview these two men. You can tell your father they're not quite right and he'll send another two. But at least you'll have bought yourself a little time for getting your dad to see your point of view."

She took a deep breath. "Right. Thanks, Jake."

She wanted to add, *Take me in your arms and kiss me like crazy the way you did yesterday so I can just sneak away from my brain for a little while.*

But that was exactly what had sent her off to the rodeo back in late January. Needing an escape from her issues with her dad. Finding it in a man's arms.

Well, hell no.

She wasn't marrying some stranger her dad was sending. And she wasn't going to forget her problems by taking off her clothes. She would face her problems. She would deal with them.

This "bring it on" attitude made her feel better and almost empowered for exactly two seconds. Because in a few hours, she'd be sitting across from Husband Candidate Number One.

Hell, yeah, Jake was sticking around to get a look at these two Suits. He was walking around with a clipboard, which was usually the foreman's thing, so he would appear as though he was doing something ranch-official while he was actually just butting his nose into Emma's business. This was his property, so technically, what happened here *was* his business.

A pricey SUV came down the drive. Jake looked at his watch. It was 1:56. Humph. The first Suit was exactly on time. Neither too early nor late.

The car stopped in the parking area, and a tall, reasonably attractive man in his late twenties got out. He, indeed, wore a suit. Jake watched the guy smooth his tie, and then check his reflection in the driver's side window. He was either obsessed with his looks or simply cared about making a good impression and wanted to be sure he didn't have a piece of corn muffin stuck in his teeth. So far, Jake had nothing bad to say about the guy, and he was hoping he could write him off before he even approached the house.

Briefcase in hand, the guy headed toward the front door.

Jake waved and walked over. "Hey there. I'm Jake Morrow, owner of the Full Circle. I understand you're here to see Emma Hurley."

"That's right," the man said, clearing his throat. He straightened his tie again. "My name is John Wellington. The third."

Jake stared him down—well, looked him over, and the man didn't flinch. Clearly not the wimpy type. "Well, follow me, Mr. Wellington."

"Everyone calls me Trey. It's French for *three* even if it's spelled the American way."

Jake raised an eyebrow. "Follow me, Trey."

"Wow," Trey said, his gaze on the small herd of cattle grazing in the nearest pasture. "Must be nice to walk outside to this kind of nature every morning. I grew up right in town, well, in Oak Creek." He took a deep breath, as if smelling the country ranch air.

Huh. Attractive enough. A third. Not wimpy. And he appreciated the ranch. Which meant he'd appreciate Emma's farm. Emma might actually go for this… husband candidate.

Jake's stomach twisted again. Was someone pinching him along his shoulders and neck?

He sighed inwardly and found himself doing the stalling by not opening the door. Not that Trey-French-For-Three seemed to care. He was smiling at how one of the bulls swatted his tail around. Dammit.

Let's get this over with before candidate number two arrives, he told himself. He opened the front door, and they stepped inside. He glanced for Emma in the living room and the game room–library. He didn't see her. Maybe she was in the kitchen, preparing cheese and crackers or something. "Emma?" he called out. "Trey Wellington to see you."

Silence.

"Emma?" he called again.

Silence.

Wellington bit his lip and looked around nervously.

"She must be in her suite," Jake said. "I'll go fetch her." Jake took the stairs two at a time. On the third floor, he knocked on Emma's door. "Emma?"

"You can come in," she called. Weakly.

He opened the door and peered in. She stood in front of the window, her back to him, her pretty light brown hair lit gold by the sun streaming in. She wore it in a low ponytail and had changed into a sundress with tiny purple flowers on it.

"This is a mockery," she said, turning around. "I can't do this."

She looked so damned pretty. And for the first time, he noticed the slight swell of her belly. She was starting to show. "You have a good plan," he reminded her. "You're stalling, Emma. Just buying yourself some time. But if you don't meet the guy, your father may think you're not meeting him halfway and he could put the farm on the market immediately."

"I'm not *really* meeting him halfway, though." She shook her head. "But if I don't go through with these stupid interviews, I lose the place that means more to me than anything. I lose my mother's family home. It's my child's legacy, Jake."

He walked over and reached up a hand to her face. He could see this was tearing her in two, breaking her heart. He'd never felt so powerless.

"My father has been trying to control me my entire life," she said. "And my entire life, I've stood up to him. But he's never threatened to sell the farm, Jake. He's won. All I have to do is marry someone I don't love in a vetted partnership. And since I'm not remotely interested in love or getting married, maybe that's not so bad, then. My baby will have a solid father figure, Reginald Hurley approved. What baby couldn't use a good father figure?" she asked, moving over to the rocking chair and dropping onto the cushion.

His stomach hurt. His collar felt very tight. He was about to jump out of his skin. He took a deep breath. Expelled it. Turned and paced the length of the bedroom. Looked at Emma. Looked out the window. Closed his eyes. Opened them and found her looking at him as though he might need medical attention. Which he might.

He paced some more, then stopped. "Marry *me*, Emma. We're both not looking for a real relationship or a real marriage. You'll save the farm."

What the hell? Had he just said that? Had he just proposed to Emma?

Good God, he had. Without thinking. *Gun to head, what are you going to do, Morrow?* Well, this was the answer.

A marriage proposal.

She stared at him. "Jake. You can't be serious. What could you possibly get out of this?"

"The best cook in Texas?" he said, managing a weak smile.

Had he just said *that*? What the hell was wrong with him? If anyone needed Emma's charm school for cowboys, he did. Good Lord.

She glanced away and sucked in a breath, then stood. "I appreciate the offer, Jake. And your kindness, your willingness to do this, is…overwhelming. But it's not the solution, either. Will you please tell Mr. Whoever that I'll be right down?"

Two-by-four right to the stomach. She was saying no? Wasn't it the perfect solution to the problem? What was he missing?

Something. Because she turned away again, this time toward the oval mirror over the bureau and she was smoothing her hair and lifting her chin. She was clearly bracing herself to meet Husband Candidate Number One.

"I'm ready," she said, giving him a tight smile. Then she marched out the door, leaving him standing there and wondering what the hell had just happened.

Chapter Six

Emma could barely walk down the stairs. Jake had proposed to her. Jake Morrow had asked her to marry him—for no other reason than to save her farm.

She knew she was a good cook, but come on. A good steak couldn't mean that much to him.

He'd proposed because he could clearly see that she was between the ole rock and hard place and there was no place soft to land—except him, not that there was anything soft about Jake Morrow's body. He was a stand-up guy, the very type of man her father would want her to marry. Gallant. Successful. Just the right this and that for the neighbors and board members.

And if Emma wasn't falling for Jake, she might even accept. Last night, when thinking about her father's ultimatum had been too much, she'd thought of Jake instead. How she'd felt in his arms at the dance.

How he'd tried to intervene with her father. *With all due respect, Mr. Hurley...* The kiss last night. The unbelievable, amazing, toe-curling kiss.

How he'd talked this through with her.

How he had moments ago proposed to save her farm.

But he didn't love her. Love wasn't part of this. He had his own life complications right now and he was focused on those and building the ranch. She'd had her heart and expectations smashed by one magical night with a cowboy. Now she'd fallen for a cowboy for all the rightest and realest reasons. And how could she risk all that pain and heartache? They'd sleep in separate beds because it wasn't a real marriage. They'd fake kiss in public and then resume their normal separate lives in private. How could she live that way? And if she married him and things blew up in their faces, her child would be left without the only father figure he or she knew and loved.

She shook her head. She wasn't playing games with her or her child's feelings and heart and future. Maybe a dry-eyed, cold deal of an arranged marriage with someone she felt nothing for was the way to go. If she had to marry to keep the farm—it was.

All that settled in her head, she reached the bottom step and saw a man standing up and watching her. Oh God, had he watched her descend like this was prom night?

He was in the living room. Certainly she wasn't going to interview him for the position of Husband right out in the open.

"Trey Wellington," he said, clutching a briefcase

with one hand and extending his other to her. He looked eager and nervous.

She forced herself to smile. "Very pleased to meet you. Let's talk out on the patio. It's a really nice afternoon."

He smiled and followed her. He had a nice enough face. Brown hair. Brown eyes. Silver-rimmed glasses. He wore a dark gray suit and had shiny black shoes. She wondered what could possibly be inside the briefcase. School transcripts? References from family and friends and neighbors?

"I'll cut to the chase," Emma said as they sat down, the big gray-and-white umbrella shielding them from the bright sunshine. "As I'm sure you know, I'm pregnant and unmarried and my father doesn't approve. He wants to find me a suitable husband and father for my baby. You're applying for this role?"

It sounded so ridiculous, so completely unbelievable that she expected Trey Wellington to get up and run out. But he just smiled and opened the briefcase and handed her what looked like a photo album.

"I certainly am," he said sincerely.

She raised an eyebrow and flipped through. It was essentially a *This Is Your Life* type account, with photos of his childhood and adulthood, transcripts from college, letters of reference and his Eagle Scout patch.

She set the album aside on the table. "Trey, can I ask honestly why you're interested in what is essentially an arranged marriage? Why not just go out there and meet someone and fall madly in love?"

"Been there, done that, Ms. Hurley. I'm not interested in going through that again. Anyway, what I really want is to move up at the firm. Your father is president and a board member. Marriage to his pregnant daughter, taking on the role as father to her child, would secure my future."

Good Lord. It was all so…unemotional. "Doesn't that seem very impersonal to you? We'd be getting *married*."

He cleared his throat and leaned a bit closer. "Your father showed me photos of you—you're lovely, if that's all right for me to say. Mr. Hurley said you could be a little headstrong but were the sweetest person he's ever known besides his late wife. So that sounded good and you do seem nice. Oh, and your dad mentioned there was the option of moving to the family farm, and I really love ranch life. So this all seems written in the stars for me."

Sweetest person he'd ever known besides his late wife…

Her father had said that?

She listened to Trey Wellington talk about how he'd always wanted a big family, five children, and that he'd love their first child, Emma's unborn baby, the same as their other four. As he went on and on about the big family he wanted, she watched his expression grow happier and happier until she realized that poor Trey Wellington was selling himself short. He was a nice guy with hopes and dreams and should marry for love. Not to secure his place in the firm.

"I do have other candidates to meet with," she said, standing up. "But you seem like a wonderful person. If it doesn't work out, Trey, rest assured that I will speak very highly of you to my father."

He beamed. "Your father was right. You are sweet. Thanks."

She smiled and walked him out to his car. When he got in and drove away, she let out the breath she'd been holding for thirty minutes.

Jake came outside, carrying a clipboard. He tipped his brown Stetson at her. "How'd it go?"

Tears unexpectedly pricked at her eyes. "My father told him I'm headstrong but the sweetest person he's ever known besides my mother."

He squeezed her hand. "That's a good sign, Emma. That means your dad may be willing to hear you. Maybe he just needs some time to digest this and he'll forget about trying to marry you off."

She blinked back the tears. Her father did love her. He was just difficult and controlling. But he clearly loved her. Yes. Enough was enough! She reached into her pocket for her phone and pressed in her father's number.

He picked up right away, clearly waiting for news on how the first interview had gone.

"Dad, it's Emma. I just met with Trey Wellington. He seems like a great guy and I hope you promote him. Look, I was wondering if you had some time to think about all this. I'm a strong-minded, capable, self-sufficient woman with a great job, a great home, and I know, without a doubt, that I'll be an excellent mother. I really don't need a husband, Dad. What I need—what I want so much—is your support. And by that I mean emotional only."

All she wanted from her father was his love. And for him to be a rocking grandpa to her child.

Reginald Hurley was quiet for a moment. Had she done it? Had she convinced him. She could barely take the silence. *Please say okay, Dad. Please.*

"I made myself clear, Emma," her father said. "Do the right thing by yourself and our family and my grandchild, or I will sell the farm."

Oh God. No, no, no. "Dad, please—"

But he'd ended the call.

Her shoulders slumped. She put her phone away, her limbs feeling like lead. She repeated her father's exact words for Jake. "So much for hoping he'd come around." She looked at the time on her phone. "Now I have a half hour before the next guy."

Jake cleared his throat. "My offer still stands."

The fact that she wanted to fling herself into his arms and scream "Save me" made her lift her chin and square her shoulders.

And the fact that he was willing to sacrifice his freedom, his future, for her was enough for her to keep saying no. She cared about him too much for that.

"Jake, I—"

"Look, Emma. I know this is all crazy. All of it. Including my out-of-the-blue proposal. So know it's an option and on the table. Let's leave it at that."

Oh, Jake. If only you knew.

Jake wasn't planning on hanging around with his clipboard to see the next guy. Based on the first candidate, he had no doubt Reginald Hurley wasn't playing. He'd picked not only reasonable guys, but ones Emma might actually like. Jake had thrown his name into the hat and for whatever reason, she wasn't jumping at it. Why? He couldn't figure that out. Seems like it would solve everything. Her father would be satisfied. She would stay here, among friends. Her life wouldn't change except on paper.

As if a legal, lifelong, binding document proclaiming them husband and wife was nothing.

Idiot. No wonder she'd turned him down. This was serious stuff and she was just stalling these guys; she had no intention of marrying anyone.

The next dude would be here in fifteen minutes. Jake forced himself away from the house. He needed to see how CJ, who'd been quiet all morning, was doing. Hank let him know CJ was out riding fence in the northern pasture. He headed toward the barn and saddled up Midnight, and then rode the gelding out toward the fence to ostensibly look for holes that needed repairing, which was mostly CJ's and Golden's jobs.

He found CJ sitting near a small hole in the fence, his tools beside him, Merlin, the gorgeous brown-and-white-spotted gelding that CJ loved, tied and grazing. CJ's head was on his arms, which rested on his knees. He was either sleeping or deep in thought not to have heard Midnight ride up.

"CJ?" Jake said.

His brother shot up and grabbed his toolbox, then kneeled down by the hole in the fence, a stretch of wire in his hand. "Just thinking about something."

"Stella?"

CJ stared at the fence. "I don't want to commit to her. But I don't want to lose her, either. What the hell do I do?"

"Well, I suppose if those are your two choices," Jake said, "then either way you lose."

"What do you mean if those are my choices. Those *are* my choices."

"But you're looking at it in black-and-white terms." Jake eyed his brother. The guy was truly torn up about this, that was plain to see. "CJ, five years ago, when I decided not to pursue finding my birth mother, I made a choice. It wasn't right then for a lot of reasons, actually. A month ago, it *was* right. Timing, all dependent on many variables, has a lot to do with decision making."

"If I tell Stella the timing isn't right now, five years from now she'll be married with two kids."

"I'm not saying you should tell her any such thing. Just that maybe you should delve a little deeper into both sides. Think about what committing to Stella would look like and what losing her would look like."

"Committing would mean not seeing any other women."

He sighed. "Right. And how do you feel about Stella?"

"Well, Stella's the most beautiful woman I've ever seen. And she can be really funny when she's not socking me in the arm. She listens when I talk too. I was telling her about how we came to move out here. About you and Sarah Mack and all that. She just let me talk, you know? Didn't tell me how to feel or what I should think. I didn't realize that until the other day."

And she sounds like a keeper, Jake wanted to say, but then he'd be telling his kid brother how to feel and what he should think, so he kept the obvious to himself. CJ would come to it. Hopefully before it was too late.

"So let's say you tell her you just aren't ready to commit," Jake said. "She's out of your life. She's dating someone else. You're seeing other women. How do you feel about her getting serious with someone else?"

"The idea makes me want to puke," he said.

Jake smiled. CJ couldn't even handle it when Stella had been late to the dance. He was going to make a decision that would cast her out of his life? Doubtful.

"My head is spinning," CJ said. "Let's change the subject. So…is Sarah helping you find the twin," he asked, his eyes on his work.

The twin. CJ couldn't even bear to say *your twin*. He wanted to grab his kid brother in a fierce hug and tell him he had nothing to worry about, that nothing would change, ever, between them. But CJ would push him away.

"I haven't started the search. I'm not sure now is the right time, anyway. We're getting the ranch going and that's consuming me, so…"

CJ turned to face him. "Yeah. We're pretty busy out here."

Every muscle in CJ's body was tight and twitching. The guy was going through some learning curves about the human condition and Jake felt for him. His brother wasn't ready—or didn't think he was, but Jake *was* ready. Dammit.

"I think about what he's like," Jake said. "Maybe he's a rancher, like us. Or maybe he's a doctor or an astronaut. Something totally different." He smiled at the idea of his twin floating in a spaceship, heading toward unexplored galaxies.

CJ was quite for a moment, then said, "Maybe he even has—" He paused and started working furiously on the fence.

Jake's smile faded. *Maybe he even has…kids? Maybe you have biological nieces and nephews?* He wondered if that was what CJ had been about to say, then had gotten choked up about it. About the idea that

Jake's biological family would include even more than Sarah Mack and a fraternal twin brother.

"Done," CJ said, standing up. "See you later," he added, getting on Merlin and riding in the opposite direction of the house.

Jake closed his eyes and tried to let the beautiful late May breeze center him. He'd thought coming up here and talking to his brother would clear his head and now everything was even more muddled.

Emma sat on the patio with Husband Candidate Number Two. Joel Wipley was also tall, also had a briefcase containing a résumé and letters of reference. He was particularly interested in showing his latest medical checkup. He was in tip-top shape with excellent blood levels.

He sat very straight, his auburn hair glinting in the sunshine. "You can bet I'll be out there in the backyard, kicking around a soccer ball with little Joel Junior or Catherine. Do you like those names? I've always wanted a junior. And I've given this a lot of thought, Ms. Hurley. Even though your baby—" he gestured in the direction of her belly "—isn't mine, I think we should go with Joel Junior if he's a boy so that he always feels like he's mine."

Emma supposed the sentiment was nice but she felt sick to her stomach. *He's not yours,* she wanted to scream. *I don't even know you*!

She let Joel Wipley go on for a half hour about how he too was very ambitious and wanted to make executive vice president before age thirty, which was two years away. He was senior director right now and had a real shot at his dream.

Finally, when she could reasonably say she'd given him long enough at a fair interview, she stood and thanked him and let him know she'd tell her father that he seemed like real executive vice president material. He beamed, and Emma showed him out through the front door.

Just as Joel Wipley got into his car, Jake was coming from the goat pen and CJ came out of the barn. She noticed Jake giving the candidate a glance as the Morrow brothers headed toward the house.

Marry me... She heard Jake's proposal over and over. She couldn't take her eyes off Jake as she adjusted his Stetson against the bright sunshine, his biceps evident under the navy blue T-shirt he wore. Her gaze traveled down his sexy jeans to his brown leather work boots. She swallowed.

It had to be the hormones. Was she actually standing here drooling over her boss's body and face? Especially when any minute now, she could expect a call from her father demanding to know which man she would be choosing as her husband and a father for her baby?

Jake tipped his hat at her as he approached, his green eyes blazing with curiosity. She knew he wanted to ask her how the interview had gone, but he wouldn't in front of CJ. Heck, CJ had opened up about his personal life, and she didn't see any reason why hers had to be a secret.

"Who was the suit?" CJ asked, glancing from the car disappearing up the drive back to Emma.

Emma didn't mean to, but she launched into the whole story.

"I'm surprised Jake didn't get on one knee already," CJ said, mock elbowing Jake in the ribs.

"You think I didn't propose? Of course I did," Jake said.

CJ stared at his brother, his mouth dropping open. "I was kidding. But I have no doubt you did. You're like that."

"Which is why of course I turned down his generous offer," Emma said, sliding a glance at Jake. "I can't let him come to my rescue. First of all, I will rescue myself. Second of all, I don't even want to get married! Third of all, there's no way I'd marry for the wrong reasons."

Jake kept his gaze on Emma but he didn't say anything. She wondered what he was thinking, if he had any idea just how complicated the thought of taking his proposal seriously was.

"So what do you think, CJ?" Emma said as they went inside and she shut the door behind the brothers. "My dad will see reason and come around to my way of thinking, right? I have nothing to worry about, right?"

CJ raised both eyebrows. "I might be only twenty-two, but I know your dad's type, Emma. Conservative. Traditional. I don't know that he *will* come around. And based on what he said just an hour ago on the phone…"

Sigh. He was right. "So what choice do I have? None. I'll have to enter into an arranged marriage. I suppose I could look at it as two adults knowing exactly what they're heading for. No love or romance but probably affection, no feelings getting hurt."

"Emma—" CJ began.

She could feel her heart ready to explode. "But I don't want to get married at all! And even if I did, how could I marry a man I don't love? How can I not marry a man I don't love and lose my mother's farm?"

She could feel Jake staring at her and she turned away.

"Emma!" CJ shouted. "I have your solution."

"You do?" she and Jake asked in unison. Their gazes swung from CJ to each other, then back to CJ.

"Can we talk while I make a sandwich?" CJ said. "I'm starving."

She glanced at Jake and he shrugged. They trailed CJ to the refrigerator where he pulled out fixings for a very big Italian sandwich. Then he opened every bread box until he found the crusty rolls he wanted.

Emma sat down at the table, fascinated by how many slices of salami CJ was putting on the roll. Jake stood next to the fruit basket on the counter. He picked up an apple and took a loud bite.

"So here's what you do," CJ said. "You get *engaged*. You two," he added, wagging a finger from Emma to Jake.

"What?" Emma and Jake said—again—in unison.

CJ reached into the refrigerator and pulled out the mayo, mustard and horseradish sauce. "You heard me. You two get engaged. That takes all these contenders off the table. And it'll get Emma's father to back off long enough for him to digest the idea that she's a modern woman who's going to have her baby on her own. When he does, you call off the wedding that never was. Emma, if you meet someone and fall in love later on, great. But right now, this is your situation."

"Huh," Jake said, taking another bite of the apple.

"Huh," Emma repeated, biting her lip. Huh. It wasn't a terrible idea. It wasn't even a bad idea. But was it a *good* idea?

CJ cut his sandwich in half. "Yeah, the engagement will be fake, but it's just an *engagement*. No vows are being broken. You're not promising to love, honor and cherish and all that scary stuff." He mock shivered, then eyed the two of them. "I'll leave you two to work out the details." He grabbed a bottle of water, then an apple and a banana from the fruit basket, and then reached into the cabinet for the pretzels. He shook some into a baggie and put it into his bag.

As CJ headed out with his lunch, Jake said, "I can't believe it, but I think my kid brother is on to something."

"I don't like lying," she said. "I'd be lying to my father."

Jake sat down at the table. "Well, here's the thing. You *are* in this situation. I offered to marry you. You said no. So now, thanks to CJ, we're downgrading it to an engagement. That's not fake. My offer wasn't fake. I would marry you to save the farm, Emma. There's no lie here."

She held his gaze, then stared down at her hands, which she kept clasping and unclasping. "Well, when you put it like that, I guess there's not. Very clear."

He nodded. "Only problem is, I proposed and you said no, so how could we be engaged?"

"I'd laugh, but I'm about to cry, Jake."

"Will you be my intended bride for the time being until this is all sorted out, Emma Hurley?" He extended a hand, palm down.

This *would* solve her problems—for the time being. Being fake engaged didn't feel great, but she had to do something. "Yes," she said, putting her hand on his.

He squeezed it. "Right now, we're doing what needs to be done. Let's just get through it best we can."

She nodded. They were doing what needed to be done. She would not allow herself to fall in love with Jake Morrow. She would just steel guard her heart.

The problem was the hormones, making her all extra emotional. Dang.

Chapter Seven

Redford, who barely tolerated anyone but Jake, curled up on the brown leather sofa beside Emma, his furry orange chin on a paw. After shaking on the new plan, Emma had suggested she and Jake take an hour or two to digest it and get together this evening to discuss the logistics.

As Jake poured apple cider into two wineglasses—the next best thing to champagne—he realized he was now an engaged man. Even though it was a fake engagement, he couldn't help but feel…what? Connected even more so. Entwined. A team. And something else that he couldn't quite put his finger on.

Jake brought the glasses into the living room and handed one to Emma, then sat on the other side of Redford. "To our engagement," he said, clinking the glass.

She didn't say anything, but at least she clinked, which meant she must be feeling a little better about having to do this.

"I think the first thing we need to discuss is whether or not we tell the crew," Jake said. "CJ knows, of course, but the more people who know that this is a fake engagement the more we might be asking for trouble. Especially when Hank has tact issues and Grizzle is honest to a fault. Golden's the only one I don't have to worry about since he rarely says anything at all."

Emma sipped her cider. "I think we should tell the cowboys. The crew has come to feel like family to me and I don't feel right keeping the truth from them."

He squeezed her hand. "It means a lot to me that you feel that way—that they're family. I look at them that way too. We'll need to hammer home that they can't talk about it or discuss it. If someone mentions our engagement, they'll just say, 'isn't that great' or something like that."

Emma put the glass down, her big blue eyes worried. "As for my dad, isn't he going to think it's awfully convenient we're suddenly engaged?"

"I've been thinking about that for the past hour," Jake said. "We tell your dad the *almost* truth. That after those Suits came and went, I decided I didn't want to lose you to a parade of candidates and so I proposed myself. You can tell your dad that we've gotten unexpectedly close since you arrived."

Funny thing was, none of that was almost true; it *was* true.

She looked at him for a long moment, then gave

Redford a scratch behind the ears. "I suppose we'll have to act engaged in public."

"I never made it to engaged," Jake said. "So I don't know exactly how that looks, but I guess a little PDA when it feels warranted. We'll have to act the part."

He suddenly pictured her beneath him in bed, naked, her long golden hair fanned out, her hands in his hair, scratching his back. Whoa. In bed, he wouldn't have to act at all. His desire for her would take over. But out in town, having lunch at Hurley's or seeing a movie—would they hold hands? Gaze longingly at each other? All stuff he wouldn't mind doing with Emma at all. All stuff that would come quite easily. He could look at Emma Hurley all damned day.

She nodded, pushing a swath of golden-brown hair behind her ear. "A kiss here and there. Holding hands on Main Street. We might have to suffer through some wedding planning too." She looked a bit sad. Maybe just conflicted.

He hated that she had to do any of this. The lie. The acting. All she wanted was to live on her own terms, and he respected that.

"But at least at home, we can retreat to our own lives," he said, hoping that would help ease her discomfort.

She glanced at him. "Right. Because everyone here will know it's just for show and temporary."

"So when is the wedding?" he asked. "We are getting married before the baby comes, right?"

Her expression changed so suddenly, so dramatically that he wanted to kick himself. Whereas before she seemed to be going along with all this just fine, or tolerating that she felt she had to go along with it, he'd added a little too much reality to make-believe. He'd brought the baby into it. *Idiot*, he chastised himself.

"That'll be the first question my father asks, I'm sure," she finally said. "So we should know how to answer it. Reginald Hurley will say that we should marry immediately. He'll like the idea that everyone will think the baby is yours."

"Except you wore a Baby on Board shirt to the dance last night," he reminded her. "The engagement is coming after."

"Yeah, I fixed one problem with the shirt—to ward off bucks' choicers—and created an ever bigger problem. Well, if my dad insists we marry right away we'll just make it clear that we want a reasonable engagement period so that we're not rushing into anything, that this is for life, this is the baby's future, and we want to make sure everything is in order before we say 'I do.'"

"I can't see him objecting to that," Jake said.

I do. He thought back to five years ago, when he'd been ready to say "I do" to Samantha. The romantic gesture of hiring the skywriter. Thinking his entire future was settled—and having no idea how that future was about to crack wide-open in so many ways. Huh. Maybe CJ was right about life being a crapshoot. You just never knew.

As in what was going on in Emma's life…she probably never saw any of this coming, despite all her father had done and said prior. Suddenly, he wanted to be by her side more than ever, there for her, a rock for her.

He supposed it was kind of nice to have her by his side too, especially now.

"I'll call my dad and let him know we're…engaged," Emma said. "He'll probably invite us over to celebrate. It'll be our first show."

She stood up so quickly that he wasn't entirely sure her face crumpled, but he was pretty sure it had. She moved to the windows overlooking the front yard and the bull pastures. He could see her reflection in the glass—including how sad she looked.

He walked up behind her and put his hands on her shoulders. "Everything will be okay, Emma. We're doing what needs to be done."

She turned around and leaned her head on his shoulder and he wrapped his arms around her. When she tilted her head up as if to say "thank you," he found her so damned beautiful that he couldn't resist leaning down to kiss her. Her lips were so soft and warm.

She kissed him back, her hands on his neck, and all he could think about now was making love to her and wondering what was underneath her sundress.

She stepped back. "Jake. Let's not make this confusing. Our relationship is crystal clear right now—we're entering into a sham engagement for a very good reason."

Right. And she wasn't looking for more. She didn't want to get married at all. And neither did he.

"I'll save it for public not private," he said.

"I don't like any of this," she said and hurried up the stairs, leaving him standing in the middle of the living room.

Oh hell, Redford, he said as the orange tabby padded past him. "I'm turning into Hank. Saying the wrong thing at the right time."

* * *

An hour later, Jake called the guys together for a meeting in the barn. He glanced at Emma, standing by Midnight's stall, wondering how they would take the news. Hank and Grizzle were both "take me as I am, take it or leave it, I speak the truth" kind of men. And Golden always did the right thing. But in this case, Emma wasn't even sure she was doing the right thing.

As Jake explained the situation, from Emma's father issuing his ultimatum at the dance to CJ coming up with the brilliant plan to fake an engagement as another stalling tactic until Emma could make her father see reason, he watched each man's face. Hank shook his head. Grizzle grimaced. Golden was slack jawed. And CJ's face was glued to his phone.

"So," Jake concluded, "no matter what, no matter where we are, no matter the situation, Emma and I are engaged. It's very important you all just go along with it, no matter what is said. Nod and smile kind of thing. No need to comment or add details. Nod and smile. Emma and I are engaged. I'm her fiancé."

"I woulda stepped up too," Hank said.

"Ditto that," Grizzle said.

"Me too," Golden said.

"I would have if I wasn't going out of my head about a woman making me choose between her and my freedom," CJ said, kicking at some errant hay. "And besides, Jake already stepped up."

No matter what anyone said about these four, Jake thought, they were the best. They might be rough around the edges, but who the hell cared? They were good people. Through and through. He could see Emma's eyes mist up and she swiped at them.

"Dammit, CJ, you made Emma cry," Hank said, shooting CJ a glare.

"No, no," Emma said. "These are happy tears. The five of you are pretty wonderful. All of you."

"Then why did Fern text me a little while ago that she never wants to see me again for as long as she lives?" Hank said, frowning.

"Uh-oh," Emma said. "I thought things were going well since you apologized after the dance!"

Hank threw up his hands. "She asked if I liked her new short haircut, and I said no, I liked it better before, and she got all mad, so I told her I knew a company that made wigs from horse hair for cheap. She stormed off. Then the text. Jeez."

Well, that was who cared about Hank Timber being rough around the edges. Fern.

"Oh, Hank," Emma said, shaking her head. "Jake and I are going to Oak Creek to see my dad in a bit, but when we get back, let's talk."

Hank's scowl deepened. "I don't get it If someone asks you a question, why isn't the truth okay? No, I don't like the shorter hair."

"Because the answer is always 'you look beautiful,'" Golden said, sheepishly looking up. "That's the answer, no matter what."

Hank narrowed his eyes. "Well, if you have all the answers, Golden, why the heck aren't you putting them to use by asking out Katie?"

Golden's cheeks flamed.

CJ looked up from his phone. "Golden's right, Hank. 'You look beautiful no matter what' is always the answer. Everyone knows that."

"Well, I'll tell you, I'm getting mighty tired of having to be on my best behavior when I don't even know what best is!" Hank shouted and marched off.

Jake couldn't help smiling. The man was being put through the wringer. But a necessary wringer.

"Poor Hank," Grizzle said, chortling.

"Poor *Emma*," CJ said. "She and my bro here have to put on a show for her dad in about a half hour. Think he'll fall for it?"

Jake glanced at Emma. But before either of them could say anything, Grizzle smirked and said, "Oh, these two will have no trouble at all."

Emma swatted at Grizzle with a grin, but Jake could see the pink on her cheeks. The comment had unsettled her. It unsettled him. That kiss last night, which maybe shouldn't have happened right in front of an undraped window at night where anyone could see, had been so real that Jake could still feel the softness of Emma's lips, how she'd felt in his arms, how right in that moment everything had seemed. But then whammo, once they pulled away it had felt so wrong. To kiss like that, to feel like that, with everyone so settled in the wrong direction. They weren't a couple. They weren't headed anywhere.

He wasn't so sure they easily *could* convince anyone they were madly in love.

As Emma turned in the driveway of her family home, her heart both quickened and sank. She loved this house. And to save it, she had to pretend to do exactly what she said she didn't want. Worse, she was faux engaged to a man she was falling more deeply in love with by the hour. A man who didn't love her. A man who'd give up his future for her. Because like CJ had said, that was who Jake Morrow was.

"This is some house," Jake said, looking up at the three-story white clapboard farmhouse with its red door and black shutters.

"The real treasure is in back," she said, walking around the side of the house on the blue stone path.

The grounds opened up into a hundred acres of land with crops and orchards. Her mother had planted the lemon trees when she herself was a little girl beside her own mother. Emma had planted the pomegranate trees with her mother's help.

One day this magical oasis will be yours, her mother had said many times over the years. *And then your own child's...*

Which was a good reminder why she was doing this, going through with this charade.

The sliding glass doors opened and Reginald Hurley stepped out. Her father was almost as tall as Jake, and about fifty pounds heavier, his imperial manner adding to how imposing he always seemed. "Jake," he said, extending his hand. "Very nice to see you again. I'm delighted by the news that you and Emma are engaged. Of course, I have two young executives to disappoint and I've canceled the two I'd planned to send over, but Emma has made her choice."

Jake shook hands with her father. Reginald Hurley looked pleased. Did it really not matter to her father if Emma was in love or happy? Did only appearances matter? It seemed so.

They walked around the grounds, Emma's father telling Jake about the orchards. She could hear the reverence and love in his voice for the farm. The thought that propriety, how things looked, could take precedence over this place was hard to believe.

Then again, despite loving this place so much and wanting to learn how to run it herself, Emma had left, unable to abide by her father's rules and regulations for her, unwilling to live life his way. She'd made a choice.

Yes, her dad was entitled to his feelings, but at her expense?

She supposed he could say the same thing about her.

Arrg, Emma thought. Why was this all so complicated?

"I had a feeling there was something between you two at the dance," Reginald said, his blue eyes twinkling—a rarity. "I could feel a certain intensity in the air. I'm not surprised to hear that my ultimatum sparked a little jealousy on Jake's part and that he proposed before anyone else could sweep you off your feet."

Did one get swept off her feet by an arranged marriage?

"Have you chosen a date?" Reginald asked. "Of course you'll want to marry very quickly."

Jake had called that one. "We were talking about an August wedding. Small and just family."

"That sounds perfect," her dad said. "I know Emma likes to take care of her own business, so you just tell me when and where to show up, and I'll be there with my dancing shoes."

Emma wanted to cry. She managed a nod, and felt Jake's arm around her shoulder. She leaned against him, needing the support. How on earth would she keep this up for as a long as it took her father to come around? And what if he never did?

"I see you haven't had a chance to go ring shopping yet, and I'm glad," her dad said, eyeing her left hand. He reached into his pocket and pulled out a black velvet box, which he handed to Jake.

"What's this?" Jake asked.

"It's to present to your bride," Reginald Hurley said. "It was Emma's mother's."

Tears pricked Emma's eyes and she blinked them away. This was going too far.

"Your mother would have wanted you to have it," her dad said, his own eyes misty.

Jake opened the box and a beautiful diamond solitaire ring gleamed and sparkled. He took the ring out and Emma slowly held out her left hand. He slid it on her finger, then held her hand.

Emma's heart clenched. This ring represented love and commitment and forever. Her mother had loved her father, despite how difficult he'd been to live with. And her father had loved her mother, compromising time and again when Violet Hurley had put her foot down. She looked at the stunning diamond on her finger and felt like a fraud.

"Violet would have liked you, Jake," Reginald said. "She held ranchers in the highest esteem. Working the land, with animals, growing crops. I couldn't be more pleased if I'd chosen you myself."

Oh, Dad, Emma thought.

Jake smiled. "Well, I'm a lucky man. Emma is a smart, independent woman who knows her own mind and she's going to be a wonderful mother."

Emma looked at Jake, touched by the chess move. He was speaking on her behalf, trying. And it made her fall even more in love with him.

"Now that she'll be raising the baby in a proper home, I'm sure she will be," Reginald said.

So much for trying. Emma stiffened, and Jake seemed to know better than to challenge that statement. Her father was conservative and set in his ways, and his mind wasn't going to be changed in one afternoon. But they were off to a good start. Her father was happy with her "fiancé." That meant he thought Emma was making good choices for herself and the baby. The higher regard her father had for what she did, the more he'd surely come around to seeing things her way.

"Thank you for Mom's ring, Dad," Emma said, barely able to look at the ring again despite treasuring it.

He leaned over for something of a hug. "I'm just glad you saw things my way," Reginald said.

Oh God. How was this possibly going to end well? And it would have to end, eventually. It wasn't like Emma and Jake would be getting married. But the baby *was* coming. At some point, her dad would insist on a wedding.

"You might be headstrong, Emma," Reginald said, "but now you're going to be a parent and parents puts their baby first."

Why can't you put me first, then? she wanted to shout.

She looked at the ring gleaming on her finger, then at the handsome man standing beside her, changing the subject to the Texas Rangers' chances for the play-offs. Part of her was very relieved that he was good at this.

But most of her was very worried at how easy it all was.

When they left Emma's father's house, Jake suggested they stop in at Hurley's Homestyle Kitchen and let the ring do the telling for them. Emma would need her great-aunt and cousins to know about the engagement or it might seem strange to her father if he discovered the Blue Gulch Hurleys hadn't been informed.

Clementine Hurley Grainger, the head waitress, walked over with menus and spotted the ring in two seconds. She wrapped Emma in a hug and shook Jake's hand and brought Emma into the kitchen. There was a lot of oohing and ahhing over the ring and a lot of congratulations and hugs. Georgia Hurley Slater whispered in Emma's ear that she'd gotten married when she was expecting and Emma could borrow her gown if she liked it. Jake noticed Emma's expression managed to tighten with anxiety and soften at the kindness.

"I'm sure your dress is beautiful, Georgia, and that's very nice of you," Emma said, squeezing her cousin's hand.

Jake glanced into the dining room to see if he knew anyone; Sarah Mack and her fiancé, Edmund Ford, were having lunch. "My birth mother and her fiancé are in the dining room," he said, upping his chin at the table by the tall, narrow window. "I guess we'll need to let them know."

"Feels weird, right?" she whispered.

"Yeah. It does. But it still doesn't feel *wrong*. Being engaged," he added. He caught her staring at the ring on her left hand. Her mother's ring. "In a way," he said, "the ring is a reminder why we're doing this."

She reached up and touched her hand to his face. "Yes," she whispered. "Exactly. I need to think of it that way instead of feeling like a big fat fibbing sneak."

He put his arm around her and held her close, and she froze, realizing that when she'd touched his face and he'd hugged her, there was no acting involved. They weren't putting on a show for the public. Those gestures had been natural.

Because you care about each other, she reminded herself.

"Ready or not," Jake whispered as they left the kitchen and headed for the dining room.

With their hands joined, they walked over to Sarah Mack's table. "You both know Emma from when she used to help out in the food truck, but she's also my fiancée," he said, holding up their hands, where her diamond twinkled.

Sarah gasped and Edmund stood, wrapping Emma in a hug.

As Emma chatted with Sarah and Edmund, who both looked so damned happy for the newly engaged couple, Jake wanted to sit them all down and tell them the truth. Now he really did know how Emma felt about lying to her father. He and Sarah Mack had a very special connection and he didn't like lying. But the more he thought about whispering the truth, the more he realized he didn't like the truth. He didn't want to be Emma's sham fiancé, even if he couldn't be the real thing. And anyway, he *was* Emma's fiancé, no matter how it came to be.

What the hell was happening to him?

Chapter Eight

When they arrived home, Emma disappeared into the kitchen, and Jake sensed she needed some time to herself. He was about to head out to the barn to check in with Hank when he noticed a light shining from the third-floor landing—from the doorway leading up to the attic. That was strange.

Jake went up and opened the door to the attic. All was quiet, but the lights were definitely on. He took the steep narrow staircase up and found his brother sitting in front of their dad's trunks, looking through old sweaters. CJ was so lost in thought and memories he didn't even hear Jake come up the stairs.

"I come up here when I need to figure something out," Jake said.

CJ started and stood up. He looked uncomfortable. "I was just looking at Dad's old stuff."

Jake was afraid CJ would bolt. He looked at the trunk, trying to give his brother a little privacy. "Remember that green windbreaker," he said, pointing at the old jacket their father used to wear everytime they went hiking.

"I'll never forget that huge buck we saw right before it started raining and we all got soaked," CJ said, smiling. "Except Dad, because he had the windbreaker and we both refused to bring waterproof jackets."

Jake nodded, lost for a moment himself in the memory of himself and CJ soaked to the bone, hair plastered against their heads, their dad shaking his head but good-humored. "We could both be pretty stubborn." He kneeled in front of the trunk. "Just clothes in this one." His gaze caught on the heavy navy wool sweater his dad always wore to go riding. "I might take this sweater, if you don't mind. Good for early mornings on the ranch."

CJ nodded. "Go ahead. Maybe I'll take the windbreaker." He slid it on and zipped it, and Jake could see that his brother was remembering old times. Then he opened up another trunk, full of their father's old navy memorabilia and the thrillers he loved to read. There was a black binder and CJ flipped through it. Copies of old documents—the deed to the ranch in Mill Valley. The title on the old red pickup. "Looks like some of your adoption papers are in here too."

"Oh yeah?" Jake said, glancing over. He had most of the records in his own files, along with his birth certificate and social security card.

CJ flipped through the papers, clipped together at the top left. He stared at a page in the middle. "Whoa. There's an index card attached to this copy of some paperwork regarding your adoption. 'Fraternal twin adopted previous day by Asher family of Houston.'" CJ handed him the papers, looking astonished.

Jake froze and scanned the card, handwritten in black ink. "The information was right here the entire time," he said. "Mom and Dad never told me about my twin—I assume because they figured it would be too much for me to handle and that if I wanted to find my birth family, I'd find out that information. But this card—I wonder if it was attached by mistake."

"I guess you have what you need to find him," CJ said. "You have a last name and a city." He turned away and started putting back the books he'd taken out. "I've been a real jerk. And selfish. If you want to find your twin, you have my blessing, Jake."

The discomfort on CJ's face was something, though. Jake knew it had always been a sore subject, but there seemed something beyond just fear of losing Jake. He thought back to his almost-fiancée Samantha saying that she had to come first. Maybe that was how it was supposed to work; your fiancée, your wife, should come first above all others, but in this case, it still didn't feel right. And even now, putting CJ first, thinking of his feelings, his heart, his psyche, meant more to Jake than seeking out his twin. CJ meant that much to him. That was just how it was.

"One day, maybe," Jake said. "But right now, we're working toward something pretty amazing here at the Full Circle, building this ranch to be what we couldn't do in Mill Valley because of our jerk uncle. I think I'd like to focus on that."

He felt CJ looking at him. Trying to read him?

Looking for assurance that Jake was okay with what he was saying?

"But, CJ, when I do look for my twin, some day, I need you to know that nothing is ever going to change. You'll always be my brother. I was there the day you were born."

"You were there when your twin was born too," CJ pointed out quietly.

The very notion sent chills up Jake's spine. "Yeah. But I never saw him again. I was there the first time you crawled and walked and got those buck teeth Mom finally got fixed. I was there when you graduated from high school. I was there when you moved out here with me."

CJ gave something of a nod, the most he could handle when Jake knew he was touched. "How'd things go with Emma's dad?" he asked, deftly changing the subject as he opened another trunk—a collection of various hats, from Stetsons to baseball caps.

"A little too well. I think it really hurts Emma to have to go through this charade to save something that means so much to her. She wants her dad to care more about her than that."

He nodded. "That's kind of how Stella feels. About us, I mean she wants me to care more about her, about our relationship, than whatever is scaring the hell out of me about committing. She thinks it might be that I don't really love her."

"Do you?"

CJ turned away and unzipped the windbreaker. He pulled out his phone to check the time. "I promised Stella I'd call her at six thirty. See you later." He headed back down the stairs.

The fact that he was unwilling to answer the question—and face whatever the answer was—was pretty telling.

Jake pulled out the papers with the index card. Asher family of Houston. He had something finally, something that felt small and huge at the same time. His twin had gone from being so intangible to having a last name and a city.

You have my blessing to find him.

Jake appreciated that. Especially because it was plain as day that CJ didn't mean it. The guy seemed to be hanging by a thread emotionally and right now, Jake was going to be an older brother and let him deal with his relationship issues before Jake would use the info on the index card.

Hell, maybe Jake liked the excuse. A reason to hold off, to put it off, despite wanting to meet the guy, to see him, to know him. What was he like? What did he look like? Who was he?

Maybe a piece of Jake was a little uncertain about that last part. Who his twin was. Who his family was. What he was like. Sometimes when you went looking for something, you didn't always like what you found.

But even when those kinds of questions hit him, when unease would trail up his neck, a bigger part of him knew—just knew—that his twin was a good guy, that something inside Jake would finally both crack open and heal when he met the man.

But right now, for both Jake and his faux fiancée, it seemed patience was the name of the game.

At five the next morning, the whole crew was in the dining room for breakfast, everyone so busy eating and trying to wake up at the same time that there wasn't much talking.

Well, everyone except for Grizzle, who was neither eating nor talking—and looked almost too wide-awake. And, if Emma wasn't mistaken, a bit… shell-shocked.

"Grizzle, you'd better put something on your plate before it's all gone," Jake said. "These pancakes are amazing," he added, smiling at Emma. "And at least grab some bacon before Hank finishes off the platter."

Hank paused mid-reach for the bacon. "What? I've only had six pieces. A serving is nine, right?"

Emma laughed. "I'll make much more tomorrow, for sure."

"Can't eat," Grizzle said, pushing around some home fries on his plate with his fork. "Michelle says I have to get all gussied up to meet her kids and their kids this weekend. Suit and tie—the works. Well, I ain't doing it."

Emma recalled what Grizzle had said about the last time he wore a suit—for his wife's funeral. Her heart went out to him.

Jake took a sip of his coffee. "We all have to put on a suit at some point. It's just a few hours to make a good impression, right?"

"You know what I've decided?" Grizzle said, getting up. "I'm done with trying to be something I'm not. You think the sheep care if my hair is combed or if I'm wearing some dumb tie that's cutting off my circulation? No. So if Michelle won't take me as I am, wild hair and jeans, too bad."

Golden looked up. "But, Grizzle, sometimes you

have to make sacrifices for other people. I mean, if you want them to be part of your life."

All eyes swung to Golden.

Grizzle frowned. "Well, Michelle can sacrifice needing me to look presentable. How's that!" He pushed in his chair and stalked out.

Emma thought about going after him, but he seemed angry in a way that told her he needed to calm down a bit first. She'd give him some time and then go see if he wanted to talk. She hated the thought of Grizzle all torn up.

"You know what?" Hank said, putting down his fork. "I'm with the Griz-man. Why do *we* have to change? Why can't the women change for us? Accept us just as we are."

"Because as you are isn't up to snuff," CJ said. "Big duh there."

"You're one to talk." Hank shot back.

CJ poked at his pancakes. "I know. I want Stella but I don't want to commit. I want her to commit to me but I don't want to commit to her. That's not right."

"You're figuring it out," Emma said to CJ. "Sometimes what you really want isn't always apparent right away."

"But why is it so much damned work?" Hank said, grabbing four pieces of bacon since Grizzle had left. "Isn't love supposed to be easy? You feel it and that's it."

Jake drank his coffee and set the mug down with a sigh. "Love is easy. But relationships are work. You can't have everything your way. And when you care about someone, you want to make them happy."

Hank seemed to think about that for a second, then

frowned. "But you can't just let yourself get trampled, either. I can barely talk around Fern. Everything I say is wrong! Grizzle has to wear a suit when it reminds him of the worst day of his life. CJ has to commit or lose the gal he loves. Golden has to actually ask his crush out if he wants to date her. I'll tell ya," he added, stabbing a pancake from the platter to his plate, "only Jake has the right idea. Fake all the way. He and Emma are just pretending to be engaged. So nothing matters. Doesn't matter what they say and do. It's not going to work out in the end cuz it's not supposed to."

Everyone was quiet for a minute.

"I still have to act the part," Jake pointed out. "If what Emma and I are doing doesn't mean anything, then I can't fake it too well. And I need to. So saying our relationship is fake is bull too. It does matter. All of it. Because saving Emma's family farm is everything to her."

Hank sank a bit in his seat. CJ was staring at Jake. Golden was nodding sagely. And Emma was sliding glances at Jake, trying to understand what he was saying. What he'd said.

He couldn't feel good about this fake engagement—apart from the *why* they were doing it. Jake had proposed to someone for real once, with love and forever in his heart, and his former fiancée hadn't been willing to wait for him, to live on his terms for the time being. This couldn't be easy for Jake.

Jake turned to Emma. "Maybe you can work your magic on Grizzle again." The subject change back to Grizzle told Emma that Jake had realized he'd been a bit too revealing. "We've got a hard morning planned, but before lunch, maybe you could talk to him about Michelle? He seems so upset about it."

She was about to say of course she would, but then remembered the very exciting appointment she had at noon. With all that had been going on, she'd almost forgotten until her cell phone calendar had reminded her with a ping this morning. Sometimes Emma loved technology. "I'll talk to him, for sure, but I can't before lunch. I have an appointment with my ob-gyn for the sixteen-week ultrasound. I'll get to listen to the baby's heartbeat."

Her baby's heartbeat. She put her hands on her belly and smiled.

"You're going, right, Jake?" Hank asked, slurping his coffee.

"Wait, what?" Jake looked at Emma, who was grimacing.

"Of course you don't need to go," Emma said to Jake. "I'm going alone."

Hank poured maple syrup on his last pancake. "Jake is your fiancé, Emma. How will it look if he's not there? What if your father hears you went alone to your baby's appointment?"

Emma sat up very straight. "I'll be raising my baby alone and I'll be going to my appointment alone. That's all there is to it."

"I don't know, Emma," CJ said, slathering cream cheese on a bagel half. "If your father hears you went alone, he'll wonder why your fiancé, your baby's new father, didn't go with you. If you're going to pull off this fake fiancé thing, you really need to do it all the way."

Baby's new father. The words echoed in Emma's head until she felt dizzy.

"Emma?" Jake asked, leaning closer. "Are you all right?"

She closed her eyes and opened them, then took a deep breath. "Yes, I'm fine. I just didn't expect the conversation to take this turn." She felt Jake studying her.

"Well, CJ is right. I'm going with you," Jake said.

She glanced at him. "Jake, honestly—" She had to go alone. She had to "start as she meant to go on," as the saying went. So why did a part of her like the idea of Jake coming? Jake beside her. Someone to share in seeing the images on the monitor, hearing the heartbeat, being excited with her. And not just someone. This man. Jake Morrow.

But Jake wasn't her baby's father. He wasn't even her real fiancé. He was her boss and he was being chivalrous and kind and wonderful because—

Because why?

Because that's who Jake Morrow is, she reminded herself for the second time that day. He was a "code of the West," kind of man. Someone who *would* sacrifice what he wanted for others. As he seemed to be doing with CJ by putting the search for his twin on the back burner. Emma wasn't sure that was right, though. Yes, CJ's feelings mattered. But *Jake* did have a biological twin brother out there in the world. And trying to pretend the whole thing didn't exist was actually pushing the two brothers farther apart, not bringing them together. Surely Jake knew that, too.

Jake sipped his coffee. "I'd like to go to the appointment with you, Emma. As your fiancé."

"As my fiancé," she repeated, the words ringing hollow.

It was a good reminder that Jake was just "doing the right thing" all around.

As the cowboys got up from the table, Emma rushed to clear their plates and the platters, needing some air. She was falling in love with a man who was giving up so much for her—except where his own heart was concerned.

If only his heart was actually involved.

Emma stacked plates along her arm, a headache forming. She thought she wasn't interested in a real marriage anyway. Suddenly she wanted Jake to be in love with her?

Hank had it wrong. Love wasn't easy at all.

Sitting across from Emma and Jake in Dr. Morgan's waiting room was a teenage girl playing a game on her cell phone. The girl had come in with her very pregnant sister and was waiting for her sister's appointment to be over. But Jake couldn't stop staring at the girl—and seeing his birth mother. Sarah Mack had been just sixteen when she'd given birth to twins. She'd been sent away to a home for pregnant teenagers and, yes, Sarah did tell Jake that she'd made a few very good friends with some other girls in her situation during that time, but for the most part, Sarah had been alone. Her babies' father—Jake's biological father—had told Sarah he couldn't be the father and had shunned her.

The strong, determined woman sitting beside him wasn't sixteen. But Emma was alone and Jake didn't like it. Part of him wished Emma didn't want to go at parenthood alone so that he could turn this engagement into the real thing—well, the real thing to a point. He would be there for her and the baby, stand by her, and be the baby's father.

But Emma didn't want that. And he had to stop thinking of her as alone in the world when she wasn't. She had him, after all. She had all the cowboys at the Full Circle. She had the Hurleys. And she had her father, again to a point.

The teen's sister appeared, full of smiles and holding an ultrasound, and the doctor called in Emma. After introductions and hand shaking and a brief explanation of what would happen, the doc squirted a jellylike substance on Emma's belly, the curve of which was getting more pronounced, and they all focused their eyes on the monitor.

Emma gasped.

Jake gasped.

"Would you like to know the baby's sex?" the doctor asked.

Emma bit her lip. "Yes, darn it. I kept thinking I didn't, that I wanted it to be a surprise, but now I want to know."

"It's a girl!" Dr. Morgan said.

Emma burst into tears. She alternated between crying and laughing. Jake squeezed her hand, unable to stop smiling like a lunatic. And unable to take his eyes off the images of Emma's daughter. That was a baby. A real, live baby. A girl.

"The heartbeat is strong," the doctor said, and the sound filled the room.

"Wow," Emma said.

"Wow," Jake repeated, taking her hand again.

But he noticed Emma looking at their entwined

hands. She took a deep breath, then removed her hand from his. Jake stepped back. She was pulling away.

You're not the baby's father, he reminded himself. *You're not Emma's fiancé. Careful how pulled in you get by the situation.* The situation being the way his heart seemed to respond to Emma Hurley. And now her baby.

"My nurse runs a free Lamaze and baby-rearing class for first-time parents," Dr. Morgan said. "If you're interested, the first class starts next week—Wednesday night."

"We'll be there," Jake said with a firm nod.

But he felt Emma glaring at him.

As they exited Dr. Morgan's office, a few people on the sidewalk nodded and smiled. *Oh, look at the nice couple coming from their ob-gyn's office.* How was it that a piece of Emma relished how good it felt to be a couple, a team, especially when she was facing something so…monumental, when another piece of her was determined to be her own woman and raise her baby herself? Why did she keep forgetting, even for a moment, that Jake being beside her was solely for show? Yes, he was a good man and seemed to care about her, and she was sure that was also why he was here. But those things didn't add up to love.

"I think I'm holding the images upside down," Jake said, turning over the pictures. "Considering your name is right there on the left, the photo goes like this. Yup, I had it upside down. Now I see the nose. Aww."

Was Jake Morrow *awwing* over her baby's nose?

Violet's nose. She was having a girl. Violet Hurley. Emma put her hand on her belly and looked up at the sky, the fluffy white clouds, sure her mother was with her and watching and liked that there would be a little Violet coming along in just a few months.

Lauren Harwood, a CPA in the office next door, was heading into her building and glanced at what he was looking at, then made her own *aww* smile at Jake and Emma.

Okay, Jake was a little too good at this. Too great at being a fake fiancé doing the things fiancés did for their pregnant brides-to-be.

And the question was: Was he even trying? Or did this come naturally? Emma didn't think Jake had to try very hard at all. He was gold. He was the kind of man that checklists were made from. Would attend baby birth and child-rearing classes: check.

"Jake," Emma said once the woman headed inside. "I don't expect you to be my Lamaze coach. I'm sure the teacher is used to a single mom-to-be. She can be my partner. Or maybe there'll be another solo student."

His dark hair was lit in copper in the sun, and he put on his Stetson to shield his eyes. "You need a Lamaze class and don't you need a partner for that? Plus it's a combined class on child rearing—why pass that up?"

But. I'll be doing it with you. And I'll feel like we're in this together. That you're my baby's father. That we're a team.

And they weren't.

"This morning I called BabyCenter and opened an account for you," Jake said as they headed toward his car. "You can pick out whatever you need—car seat, diapers by the truckload, clothing."

She stopped walking. "Jake, I'm perfectly capable of supporting my child. I can buy my own bassinet."

"Emma, I'm just—"

"Just trying to help. Just trying to be a good fiancé. Just trying to do what's expected," she finished for him. "But when all is said and done, I'm going to be on my own. I have savings, I have a salary. I can pay for whatever I'll need for the baby."

"The—" he began.

"Oh, thank God," a familiar voice interrupted.

Emma turned to see Hank carrying a brown-and-white puppy with floppy ears. Whatever Jake had been about to say—to argue—was lost as they admired the adorable little dog.

"How cute!" Emma said, taking a step back. "I'm allergic, but I know adorable when I see it."

"CJ and Golden are both allergic too," Jake said. "So we can't have dogs at the ranch, Hank. You know that."

"It's not mine!" Hank said. "It's Fern's! The little squirmer ran off from the box she was bringing into the shelter. She found the pups abandoned on her farm."

"Well, it's good that she's talking to you again," Jake said.

Hank frowned, giving the pup's brown-and-white head a nuzzle. "Actually, I just overheard the conversation. So what do I say when I bring the pup over to her? I want to make things right."

"I thought you were tired of working so hard to say the right thing," Jake said, a teasing glint in his eyes.

"I am, but look at her—she's beautiful," Hank said, his entire body drooping with love as he stared over at Fern, who had run out of the shelter, clearly looking for the missing pup. Fern, in her late thirties, had curly long auburn hair just a bit darker than Hank's, her pretty face covered in freckles. She was as petite as Hank was tall, and both were partial to tan Stetsons.

"Just go over there with the puppy before she starts hyperventilating," Jake said, giving the puppy a pat under the chin. "Be yourself."

Hank narrowed his eyes at Jake. "What? Now I'm supposed to be myself?"

"Let your feelings guide you, Hank," Emma said, hiding her smile. It wasn't easy.

"Humph," Hank complained and jogged over to where Fern was knelt down in front of the bushes by the shelter.

Emma watched Fern shoot up, relief crossing her face. She took the puppy and nuzzled him, then wrapped her arms around Hank in what looked like a thank-you hug.

And then she kissed him on the cheek.

Hank touched his fingers to the spot. Aww. You couldn't fake that reaction.

They spoke for a minute, and then Fern went back inside and Hank jogged back over.

"We have a date tomorrow night at Hurley's!" Hank said. "It worked!"

"What did you say?" Jake asked.

"I told her I found the little runaway and that I was kinda glad he ran off so that I could catch him and do her a favor because I like her so darn much but always say the wrong thing. And she said, that was just the right thing. So I risked asking her out and she said yes."

Emma grinned. "I'm very happy for you, Hank."

"Good work," Jake agreed, and then Hank sauntered off to his truck, whistling a country tune.

"Speaking of saying the wrong thing," Jake said. "By opening the account at BabyCenter, I just want you to have everything you want."

"I appreciate that, Jake. But I earn a salary. You know that. I can pay my own way."

"I know but—"

"I don't need to be rescued," she said. "Why can't you understand that?"

"Emma, helping isn't rescuing. It's helping. Did Hank rescue Fern by helping catch that puppy? Come on."

"You're infuriating!" she said. "You don't understand."

"I'm not your father, Emma. I'm not trying to control you. I just *care.*"

"Then let me be who I am."

"Who you are is very stubborn, though," he said, his expression softening. "You have to admit that's true."

"Stubborn, or determined to live on my own terms? Given how we're trying to help the cowboys change who they are for their own good, you seem to think I'm acting like my own worst enemy here. That's not fair."

He put a hand on her shoulder. "I'm just saying you don't have to go it alone. You're not alone. Yes, some people in your life need boundaries. I don't dispute that. But don't push everyone else away because you think accepting help means weakness or that you're lying to yourself."

"I need to run an errand," Emma said, eyeing the supermarket down the street. What she really needed was to escape Jake's presence for a good fifteen minutes and let all this sink in. Suddenly, it was too much—that he'd come to the appointment. That he'd found out with her that she was having a baby girl. That he seemed to know her so darned well.

"Me too," he said. "Why don't we meet at the car in a half hour."

She nodded and hurried across the street, sure he was watching her. When she turned to see if he was, he was, and he held up a hand in a wave, then finally turned himself and walked up Main Street.

Why was he so damned...dependable? Trustworthy. *There.*

She went into the supermarket, the air-conditioning refreshing. She stopped in the produce section and grabbed a basket, loading it up with fruit and vegetables.

"Oh, ma'am, let me!" a clerk said, taking the basket from her. "I'm happy to get you a cart so you don't have to carry this in your condition."

What about me says I can't carry my own basket of apples and kale! Emma wanted to shout, but then she glanced at the kind, smiling teenage clerk hurrying for her basket. People were just nice. And she should appreciate it. Jeez.

Emma smiled. "Thank you. That would be nice. I didn't realize I'd be buying so much."

Humph. Maybe Jake was right. A little. Maybe she had to chill out a little.

But if she accepted too much from Jake, she'd want it all. His love. His heart. His arm around her forever. And that was going too far for him.

Chapter Nine

As Emma set the five perfectly cooked steaks on the platter and turned off the grill, she was struck by the thought of herself doing exactly this not very long ago on the day she'd come to the Full Circle Ranch. That day, Jake had been a total stranger, a hot man in an apron and holding tongs, chasing after a goat. And Emma had come to find her baby's father to finally tell him he was going to be a father.

Now that stranger had become not only her faux fiancé, but a man who seemed to want to live up to that title of father. The ultrasound appointment. The joy in looking at the image. The need or want—whatever it was—to outfit a nursery for her. Jake Morrow had hired her when she'd been unmoored, given her a job she loved at a place she loved with people she was beginning to care deeply about. He was making himself indispensable to her, and Emma couldn't afford to need or rely on anyone.

When she brought the steaks to the table, the cowboys were sitting down. She felt Jake watching her, trying to assess whether she was still prickly about their discussion earlier. They'd agreed to shelve it on the drive back home from town, then had gone their separate ways for the next couple of hours.

"Mmm, mmm!" Grizzle said, sniffing the air. Those steaks smell amazing. And I love these roast potatoes you make with that spicy spice."

"It's called garlic," CJ said, rolling his eyes.

"Well, la-di-da." Grizzle shot back. "Whatever, I like 'em." He served himself a heap of the potatoes.

"Thanks, Grizzle," Emma said, sitting down. She was craving steak like crazy and filled her plate. The potatoes *were* delicious, if she did say so herself.

"Um, Emma?" Golden whispered, spearing two stalks of asparagus from the serving dish onto his plate. "Can I ask you something?

Emma looked across the table at the blond cowboy. "Sure, Golden."

"Tonight the rancher's association is holding a special extra Ladies' Choice fund-raising dance," Golden said. "I think Katie might ask me to dance."

"Jeez, Golden, she's probably married with a kid by now," Hank said with a snort.

Golden gave Hank something of an eye roll but smiled, then turned back to Emma. "I ran into her in the bookstore. She asked me if I was going and I said yes, well, I nodded it, and she said it was ladies' choice so I should expect to be on my feet."

"God, why doesn't she just propose," Grizzle said, laughing. "Save the both of you from this torment."

Golden's cheeks turned pink. "I guess I don't even get why she seems to like me."

"I know why," Hank said, slicing his steak and raising a forkful in the air. "Inexplicable chemistry."

"Say what?" Grizzle said. "Inexpawha?"

"Chemistry," Emma said with a nod. "That you can't necessarily explain or that doesn't necessarily make sense to anyone, including yourself. You just feel it. That special something. That zing whenever you see or even just think about the other person."

Emma glanced at Jake, sitting at the head of the table looking so impossibly sexy in his dark blue shirt. *All the things I feel when I think and look at you, that's chemistry.* Though hardly *inexplicable* chemistry. Emma could come up with a list pages long of why she was drawn to Jake Morrow.

"So she likes me even though she doesn't know me?" Golden said. "What if she gets to know me and doesn't like me then?"

Hank pointed his fork, stabbed with asparagus, at Golden. "Forget the what-ifs! You can what-if yourself to kingdom come. Katie likes you, man. *Go with it.*"

"Golden, I actually have to agree with these old-timers," CJ said. "You have *nothing* to worry about. Trust me."

Grizzle snorted. "You wish you knew half of what I know about life, CJ."

"Will someone pass the salt?" Hank said, holding out his hand. Jake shot the saltshaker down toward Hank, who caught it. "Hey, Grizzle, you still being a stubborn old coot or are you gonna let Emma fix you up again for the dance?"

"I'm sticking with stubborn old coot," Grizzle said, his hair poking up every which way. "Either Michelle takes me as I am or I guess it's over between us."

"Grizzle, you're cutting off your nose," Hank said.

"What?" Grizzle looked at Hank as though he had two heads. "Why would I cut my own nose off?"

"It's a saying," CJ said. "Cutting off your nose to spite your face. Meaning you're just hurting yourself to hurt yourself. You won't spiff up for the dance, even though you should because it's a dance. So Michelle will think you're saying she's not worth it, which means she'll dump you."

"I ain't saying that!" Grizzle said, frowning. "She's worth it. I just like how I am just fine."

Hank shrugged. "Well, I'm not taking any chances on messing things up with Fern. I've been practicing lines. Like if Fern asks how she looks tonight, instead of just saying, 'you look normal' or 'you don't have anything in your teeth,' I'm going to say, 'Fern, you look very nice.'"

Emma smiled. "That sounds perfect."

"Grizzle, maybe you're just not ready for a relationship," Hank said.

"Oh, suddenly you're Dr. Phil?" Grizzle snapped.

"It has been five years," Golden said quietly. "I hope you don't mind my saying that, Grizzle. But five years is a long time. Man, I wish I was like you guys and could just ask out the woman I can't stop thinking about. You don't know how lucky you are."

"Wise words," Jake said, nodding at Golden.

Grizzle grimaced and crossed his arms over his chest, but he didn't dispute what Golden had said.

"Still, not ready is not ready," CJ pointed out. "You have to respect that."

"Or sometimes not ready is unwilling," Jake said.

CJ glanced at Jake and spooned some potatoes on his plate.

Unwilling. Emma thought back to her argument with Jake in front of the doctor's office. Another sign they were a happy couple. Happy couples argued sometimes. But was she as stubborn as Jake said she was? *Was* she unwilling to let people help? Or did she simply want to pay her own way, be her own woman, take care of her responsibilities?

She'd accepted his help with one huge obstacle: her father. And now he was her fake fiancé, acting like a real fiancé.

Where all this was going to lead was what had Emma worried. Heartbreak.

Two slow songs had come and gone. Emma stood beside Jake, at first so relieved that no one would ask her to dance, that she held all the asking power and would not use it. But because Jake Morrow was six foot two and muscular and two inches from her side and smelled like masculine soap, she was losing the battle to keep her mouth closed. Just one simple "Dance?" and she'd be in those strong arms, her head against his rock-hard chest, his hand at her waist. She would close her eyes and lose herself in fantasy. But the more she let herself actually have the fantasy, the more real she'd wish it was. That this man was hers for real, for keeps, forever. And then she'd fall into this conversation with herself about how Jake Morrow was a good man and if she was going to let herself lean on someone, against someone, accept what was being offered, he was her guy.

Except he wasn't offering anything but his good-guy-ness. Jake Morrow wasn't in love with her. He wasn't looking for a wife for real. Even if she did let herself follow her feelings, she'd end up nowhere but alone and hurt. She wasn't starting out motherhood with a broken heart, no sirree. And so she kept her mouth closed and did not ask him to dance, especially when the band began playing her favorite Adele song.

The good news was that word had spread that the new rancher in town, the very handsome eligible bachelor Jake Morrow, was off the market and engaged to his cook. So not one woman had asked Jake to dance. Emma wouldn't like it one bit to see Jake holding another woman.

"So are we not going to continue our conversation from earlier this afternoon?" Jake asked.

She tilted her head. "About my refusal to shop at BabyCenter with your credit card as though I'm not capable of supporting my own baby?"

"Emma—" He stopped. "No. There should be no 'Emma, but' about this. This is your baby and your life and your decision."

That was unexpected. Just when she thought she had some ammunition for trying to keep herself from falling harder for him, he did just what she needed. Grr.

"Right," she said, nodding. "I'm glad we understand each other."

He held her gaze and she could tell what he was

thinking. Which was: *I'm not sure we do understand each other.*

"Let's hit the refreshment table," he said after a moment. "They have those little pigs in a blanket I can't resist. And I see Golden hiding behind a pole next to the punch bowl. And there's Katie looking all around for him," he added, upping his chin by the exit sign. "Let's get those two on the floor."

Emma smiled. "I like this mission. Operation Romance. I've got an idea. You start chatting up Golden. I'll start chatting up Katie. We inch closer and closer together. Then whammo. They're dancing."

"Aye, aye, Captain," he said with a grin.

They headed over, Jake managing to bring Golden to the refreshment table just as Emma and Katie arrived.

"Who can resist these tiny biscuit-covered hot dogs?" Jake asked, popping one in his mouth.

"Would you like one, Katie?" Golden asked, picking up the plate and holding it out to her.

Except the poor guy's hand was trembling and he dropped the plate. There were only four or five little hot dogs on it and they rolled every which way. Luckily the band was playing so loud the metal platter's clang onto the floor hardly made a sound.

Golden turned bright red and kneeled down to pick it up just as Katie did. They each had a hand on the plate.

"Now you have to dance with me, Golden," Katie said. "It's a rule. If you drop a plate of pigs in a blanket while the band is playing a ballad, you have to dance. Everyone knows that."

"True," Emma said. "It's on the list of rules posted on the door.

Jake nodded. "You'd better get out there."

Golden smiled and Katie grabbed his hand.

"What's your real name, anyway?" Katie asked.

"It's Charlie," he said.

"Charlie." Katie smiled. "I know everyone calls you Golden and that lots of cowboys go by nicknames, but I'd like to call you Charlie, if you don't mind."

He grinned. "That's fine by me." He held out his hand and Katie's took it, and off they went to the dance floor.

"This is off to a very good start," Jake whispered to Emma. He turned to look at Golden and Katie. "Come on, Golden," Jake murmured "Don't choke, don't run. Just dance. Be Charlie."

Emma squeezed Jake's hand and they both seemed to hold their breaths as Golden froze for a moment, but then he placed a hand on Katie's shoulder and they started dancing. Yes! They were dancing!

Golden wasn't choking and fleeing. He was dancing very slowly, but dancing nonetheless.

"We rock!" Jake said, picking up Emma and swinging her around. His gorgeous green eyes widened and he set her down. "I didn't hurt you or the baby, did I?"

She laughed. "Not in the slightest. And I'm happy for him too. Go, Golden!"

"Have you seen Grizzle?" he asked, glancing around. "I wonder if he's even coming. I hope so."

Emma looked around the crowded hall and easily spotted him, his hair as it was at dinner, standing up in every direction like his beard. "There he is," she said, gesturing by the edge of the stage. She watched Grizzle grimace and looked over at where he was frowning. Michelle was dancing with another man. "Uh-oh."

Jake followed the direction of her gaze. "Well, I guess Grizzle's going to have to work this one out for himself. Sometimes you have to change, even if it hurts a little, to make room in your life for someone else. Changing his hair, wearing a suit when it's called for—that's not about his late wife's memory. That's about Grizzle maybe living in the past. I understand, but it might not be doing him any good."

"If he *wants* Michelle in his life," Emma said.

"If," Jake agreed.

"Well, sometimes, a person has to stay true to himself. Or herself," Emma said. "And not let others run roughshod on them. Don't you agree?"

He looked into her eyes. "Like we've *both* said, I think people can often be their own worst enemies, make thing harder on themselves out of stubbornness or to prove a point."

"Prove a point to whom?"

"Themselves? Someone else?"

"Like their father?" she said, frowning.

He took her hand and led her away from the crowds to a quiet area where no one could overhear them. "Emma, to be honest, I don't think you're trying to prove anything to your dad. I don't think this is about him at all. I think this is about *you*. You felt betrayed by Tex—twice, and you shut down. You don't want to let anyone in and help you. You want to be strong and raise this baby on your own. That's not about standing on your own two feet. That's being scared to accept that people do love you, do care about you."

"Oh, so my father cares about me? That's why he

threatened to sell my mother's farm? That's why he tried to arrange a marriage for me? That's why I'm engaged to you?"

"Your dad thinks he's doing what's best. He's dead wrong, but it's what he thinks. I think the reason you haven't spent much time trying to change his mind is that you've realized you don't *want* to go at life alone."

"So you think I'm biding my time until you have to marry me?" she asked. "How dare you! You think this is some kind of trick to get you down the aisle, Jake Morrow?"

"What? No! That's not what I meant at all."

"Goodbye!" she said and turned on her heel.

"Emma, stop being so pigheaded for one moment," Jake said.

Emma turned back and glared at him.

"Wow, Jake is channeling the old me," Hank said, passing by as he dipped Fern at the edge of the dance floor. "Women do *not* like to be called pigheaded."

Oh hell.

When you started getting advice on women from Hank Timber, you knew you were in big trouble.

Jake watched Emma march to the door and push it open. She sure was angry. He sighed and downed a cup of the too-sweet punch. Chasing after her wasn't a good idea. He'd meant what he said, which meant he couldn't apologize—or apologize the way Emma would need him to. He had to let her cool down and give himself a minute to look at this from her point of view.

He shouldn't have called her pigheaded. Hank was right about that.

Okay, he'd start there. And they'd talk this through.

As Jake weaved his way to the exit, he saw CJ and Stella on the dance floor, Stella's head on CJ's chest for a slow pop ballad. They both had blissful looks on their faces, their eyes closed. Good for them. Golden and Katie were still dancing, and Jake had even seen Golden's lips moving, which meant all good things for the two of them. Fern and Hank had won first place in the square dancing contest, the ribbon proudly pinned on Fern's yellow top. Only Grizzle seemed miserable like Jake was, standing with his arms crossed, snacking on the new platter of pigs in a blanket and a big bowl of chips while watching Michelle ask other men to dance.

At least three of the crew were having a good time.

When he arrived home ten minutes later, his head was clearer. He found Emma curled up on the outside sofa, a blanket around her and Redford snoozing at her side. Did she have any idea how beautiful she looked under the moonlight and stars, her golden hair around her shoulders?

"I'm sorry," he said. "I shouldn't have called you pigheaded. I shouldn't even be making declarations about your life and your choices."

She whirled around. "You didn't have to leave the dance."

"Dances aren't my thing. I go for the Rancher Association fund-raising aspect. And besides, you left. Mad at me."

She smiled. "Well, I'm still mad at you but I appreciate your apology. Though I suppose I *can* be pigheaded. But only when I know I'm right."

They both laughed and he sat down across from

her. The tension in the air dissipated yet somehow, a second later, a different tension hung between them. He wanted to break through it and scoop her up in his arms and kiss her. But he held back.

He stood up and looked out at the night, at the dark pastures. There was so much he wanted to say. So much he wanted—needed—to explain. About the way he felt. About how much he cared about her, *for* her. How much he wanted her. He'd never forgotten how he'd felt that first day when she'd come to the ranch looking for her baby's father—only to have to hear, from him, that he was dead. From that moment he'd been filled with an intense need to take care of Emma, make sure she had everything she wanted, make sure her baby would want for nothing and then some.

But along the way, that sense of responsibility had deepened into something even more intense, something that was beginning to feel a lot like *love*. Not obligation.

He turned around to face her, hoping the right words would come. "I owe you so much, Emma. You and your baby. Because of Tex—Joshua. A truck backfired and spooked the mare he'd been riding on and it took off and threw Joshua."

She gasped.

"He was my ranch hand. He died on my land, working for me," Jake said, his chest seizing up. "Twenty-seven and gone, just like that." He hung his head, the weight of the loss pressing so heavily he had to suck in a breath.

"So you feel that you owe me because of that," she said quietly.

Well, yes. He did. Still—it was a hell of a lot more

complicated than that. But at least it might help her understand why he was so determined to give Baby-Center his credit card information. Taking care of that baby, starting a trust, a college fund—hell yeah, he was doing all that.

"Emma, look, I—"

She stood up and turned away, then slowly faced him, her arms across her chest. "Jake, I'm going to schedule some time with my dad tomorrow and talk to him, hopefully win him over to my way of thinking. That way, you and I can go back to being on our own."

He had to stop arguing. He had to let her go and be who she was and do what she wanted. She couldn't make it any clearer that she didn't want a real relationship.

"Good luck," he said. And then he turned around and headed upstairs.

In bed that night, Emma tossed and turned, unable to sleep, unable to stop thinking about what Jake had said. Why did her heart feel as though it was broken in two?

Duh. Because you love him. And because he just told you why he's been "Jake Morrow" where you're concerned. Because he feels guilty. He feels like he owes you for the loss of your baby's father.

Tears slipped down her cheeks and she wished Redford were beside her to cuddle.

Suddenly, everything made sense.

She stared at her left hand, her mother's beautiful diamond twinkling in the darkness. Tomorrow she would work on her father—no, not work on him; she would talk to him. She would simply lay out her case, bring her financial documents to show that she could certainly afford to raise her child on her own, that she had a great living-work situation at the Full Circle with a great group of cowboys.

So she was going to convince her father to let go of his stubborn mindset where his daughter as a single mother was concerned, and then what? She'd continue to live one flight above Jake? Work for him? How on earth could she do that? She'd have front and center seats to his life, to watching him with other women, girlfriends, a wife.

She was getting ahead of herself. Right now, well, tomorrow morning, she had to gather her documents and her wits and really think about the important details that highlighted her case—that she was a capable, determined, strong person who could go at parenthood alone.

She wasn't so sure her father would listen or hear her anyway. But she had to try. *Trying* was all she had.

Emma closed her eyes, trying to drift off now that she'd settled her mind. But the face of a handsome rancher with gorgeous green eyes and thick dark hair kept floating through her thoughts.

Chapter Ten

Since today was her day off, Emma hadn't set her alarm and was glad to see she'd slept till seven. She'd needed to catch up on her rest and it had taken her forever to fall asleep last night.

After a hot shower, she dressed in jeans and a long-sleeved blue T-shirt and went downstairs, hoping she wouldn't run into Jake. She didn't want to be reminded of their conversation. But she was starving and craving a bagel with cream cheese and a cup of herbal tea.

As she headed into the kitchen she heard voices coming from the dining room. She could smell pancakes and bacon, though someone had cleaned up the kitchen.

"You didn't do much dancing last night, Griz-man," she heard CJ say as she plunked a cinnamon raisin bagel in the toaster.

"Her loss," Grizzle grumbled.

"Is it?" Golden asked. "I danced to twelve songs last night. All this time I was sitting on the sidelines, it was *my* loss."

"Not the same thing," Grizzle said, frowning. "Katie seems to like you just as you are. Michelle wants me to change. Well, forget it."

"Grizzle, combing your hair and wearing a suit when the situation calls for it isn't about changing you. It's about you making an effort to join the world," CJ said.

"If y'all keep talking so much I'm gonna eat all the bacon," Grizzle muttered.

Her bagel toasted and her tea steeped, Emma went into the dining room and sat down next to Grizzle. He did not look happy. She offered a smile around the table at the five cowboys, surprised to see them all here at an off-hour. She felt Jake's eyes on her as she sipped her tea, forcing herself not to look at him.

I feel like I owe you...

Hank grabbed a few pieces of bacon off the serving dish. "I beat Golden in the number of dances danced. Fern and I cut up the rug to twenty-five songs. It won us the ribbon."

Emma smiled. "I'm glad you and Fern are so happy."

"I guess Jake will need some pointers from me," Hank said, his chest puffing up.

Jake rolled his eyes, but smiled at Hank and sipped his coffee.

"Uh-oh," Grizzle said, looking from Jake to Emma. "You two fighting already? You're not even engaged for real."

"Everything is fine," Jake said.

"Just fine," Emma agreed. "Golden, I'm glad you and Katie danced so much. You must have had a great time."

"I did," he said. "In fact, guess who has a date tonight at Hurley's Homestyle Kitchen? I called to reserve that little round table that faces the mountain range. Clementine said she herself would wait on us to make sure our date went perfectly."

"Aww," Emma said. "I'm thrilled for you."

Golden whispered something in Grizzle's ear. Grizzle nodded. "Oh, Emma, we have a surprise for you," Golden said. "It's in the workshop behind our quarters."

"A surprise for me?" Emma said, reaching for a slice of bacon.

Hank stood up. "Come on. We'll all show you."

Emma quickly munched her bacon, then looked at Jake and raised an eyebrow, but his expression gave nothing away. She followed the five men to the workshop behind their living quarters.

The moment she walked in, she gasped.

It was a nursery. A complete nursery. A wooden crib, painted a soft yellow with tiny white stars stenciled along the edges. A wooden mobile with tiny colorful toys hanging above it. A white wooden rocking chair with a plush yellow pillow and matching ottoman. A white bookcase with yellow stars and a matching changing table with a pad.

"You made this," she said to Golden, her mouth hanging open.

"We all did," Golden said. "Jake and CJ made the

crib. Hank and I made the chair and ottoman. And Grizzle made the mobile and bookcase."

The cowboys smiled at her, Jake hanging back a bit against the wall.

"We tried to figure out how to make a rug," Golden said. "But it would have taken forever. Something about a latch hook?" He shrugged.

"I'm beyond touched," Emma said, tears prickling the backs of her eyes. "I'm *verklempt* as my old neighbor used to say. I can't even speak." She looked at the beautiful pieces and shook her head. "You all did this for me?"

"You're one of us," Hank said. "Well, not a cowboy. Or a man. But you know, part of the crew."

"And by part of the crew, he means family," Grizzle said. "Not just an employee."

"At first we wanted to make you all this stuff in Tex's memory," Hank said. "I mean, none of us knew him too well since we only worked with him a week, but we sure did like him a lot and he was a hard worker and was always rattling off the most interesting facts. Like about how much water clouds hold before they open up. That kind of thing."

Emma smiled. She thought about the moment she'd met Joshua, the cute rodeo rider waiting in line in front of her at the refreshment stand. "The whole reason I started talking to Joshua—Tex—was because he was telling someone all about the best Texas barbecue and how it should be made, and his friend was telling him he was wrong. Well, I know about Texas barbecue and I sided with Joshua. We didn't stop talking for hours after that." She glanced at Jake, who was staring at the ground. "But Hank, you said 'at first' you wanted to make this all in Tex's memory. What did you mean by that?"

"Oh, just that it might have started that way but then we did it because you're one of us. You're Emma, not the woman Tex left behind with a baby on the way. You know?"

Emma was even more touched than she'd been a moment ago. She nodded. "I know exactly what you mean. And thank you. Thank you all."

Her gaze stopped on Jake. She wondered if he would have said something along those lines had she not disappeared up to her room last night. Maybe he'd offered her the job because she'd been Joshua's left-behind pregnant ex, but maybe he'd done everything else because she was Emma. Because of how he felt about *her.* Maybe all that had nothing to with what he "owed" her. She felt like she *knew* Jake Morrow. And she believed that with all her heart. The man did care about her, no matter what.

Emma walked over to the mobile, attached to the crib by a movable wooden arm. She touched the soft, colorful little stuffed animals.

"Grizzle made the stuffed things for the mobile," Golden said.

"Michelle helped me with the patterns, I admit," Grizzle said. "Before she dumped me, anyway."

Emma touched Grizzle's arms. "Well, Michelle must care about you to have helped out. Please thank her for me. I love the little animals."

Grizzle waved a dismissive hand, but Emma could tell the man was glad to have a reason to seek out Michelle.

"We'll get it all moved upstairs this afternoon,"

Hank said. "You can tell us where you want everything."

"You guys are the absolute best. Just the best."

They did this because they liked her. And cared about her and little Baby Violet. They didn't do it because she couldn't afford to furnish her own nursery or because they felt they owned her something. They did it simply because they cared and there was nothing else attached to it—no conditions, no strings.

It was about the nicest thing anyone had ever done for her.

Aside from proposing to her to save her farm. Jake hadn't done that out of guilt or because he felt he owed her. She knew that now with absolutely certainty.

Oh, Jake, she thought, *you wonderful, speak-your-mind guy. How can I hold you to this sham engagement and keep you from going forward with your life?* She had to talk to her dad. She had to get him to see things her way.

So Jake could carry on. Without her. So that he could find love and have a future with a woman he chose.

How she would say goodbye to him, she had no idea.

Essie switched around Emma's work schedule, so she arrived for her lunch shift at Hurley's Homestyle Kitchen at eight thirty, a half hour early. She'd needed to get out of the ranch house, away, but somewhere she felt safe and on solid ground, which meant her aunt Essie's. The apricot-colored Victorian was quiet, and her great-aunt was alone in the big country kitchen when Emma arrived.

After a hug and a glass of Essie's homemade peach smoothie, Emma got to work on today's lunch special, meatloaf and garlic mashed potatoes with two kinds of gravy.

"Did you know my meatloaf recipe was handed down from your grandmother?" her great-aunt said as she chopped onions so fast and so finely that Emma was mesmerized for a moment.

Emma chopped a bunch of stalks of celery, then grabbed a handful of garlic bulbs. "My grandmother?"

"Your dad's mom. Vanessa. She'd have us over for dinner every now and then and her meatloaf was unbelievable. My own mother and grandmother were good cooks, but I didn't know plain old meatloaf could taste like that until I tried Vanessa's. She gave me the recipe and I've never changed one tiny thing."

Emma smiled. "Is the famed meatloaf recipe from *his* side of the family the reason my father thought he could advise you about the restaurant?"

"Oh yes," Essie said with a laugh. "That and a whole slew of reasons. Your dad means well." She gave something of a devilish smile. "In his own mind, anyway."

Emma laughed, but her smile quickly faded. "He sure does think he knows what's best for me, even though I'm a grown woman."

"You're good at standing up to him," Essie said. "That's what you have to do when someone is trying to run your life."

Emma stared at the heads of garlic and out of nowhere, she burst into tears. Essie came over and sat her down and Emma poured out the whole story. The argument about her life choices that had propelled

her to the rodeo for an afternoon of forgetting everything. Meeting Joshua Smith, though that part Essie
knew. Her father's reaction to the news of Emma's
pregnancy and situation. The Baby on Board tank top
and the dance her father had crashed to find her. The
ultimatum.

"He actually sent husband candidates to the ranch?"
Essie said, shaking her head. "I'm shocked but not
surprised in the slightest. That is Reginald Hurley,
all right."

Emma took a deep breath. A sip of her peach
smoothie. A bite of biscuit with apple butter. And then
she told her great-aunt the part about Jake proposing.
Her not accepting. CJ's idea for the fake engagement.

"Ah, now some things make sense that I couldn't
put my finger on," Essie said. "I was a little confused
because the relationship between you and Jake Morrow seemed to escalate awfully fast, but then I saw
you together—here, then at the past two dances—and
I could see you both love each other."

"What? What do you mean? The engagement is
fake."

Essie raised an eyebrow. "The impending nuptials
might be fake. But the feeling between you and Jake,
the emotion, is not. I've been around seventy-six years,
Emma. I've recently watched my three granddaughters marry. I know love when I see it."

Well, the love her astute great-aunt was seeing was
all Emma's. Jake didn't love her.

She felt Essie Hurley studying her. It was as if the
woman could read her mind. "Emma," Essie said.
"Why do you think Jake proposed to you?"

"Well, at first I thought he did it because he's just

a great guy," Emma said. "And he is. But yesterday I found out he also feels he owes me because he was Joshua's boss and Joshua died on the job. I don't think that's the only reason he proposed, but I do know it's tangled up in why."

Essie took Emma's hand and held on to it for a moment. "The man stepped up the way he did because he loves you, Emma. Men do the right thing for all kinds of reasons. But underlying it all is love."

"All four of the cowboys at the Full Circle said they would have stepped up," Emma pointed out.

"Yeah," Essie said. "For the fake engagement. You said Jake proposed *marriage* before his brother ever brought up the idea of a phony engagement to stall your dad. Those cowboys care about you, absolutely. But Jake Morrow *loves* you."

Emma knew her great-aunt was very wise. But Jake Morrow did not love her. He cared about her, was all. Jake Morrow was the kind of man who'd put off looking for his own biological twin brother to spare the discomfort of CJ. He was the kind of man who'd propose marriage so that she wouldn't have to marry one of her father's vetted husband candidates in an arranged marriage that would destroy her soul.

Emma hugged her aunt for making her feel better, for listening, and the kitchen crew began filing in, so they got back to work. But all Emma could think about was Jake asking her to marry him. Kissing her. Looking at her in a way that send jolts up every nerve ending. Helping CJ make her baby's crib and keeping the workshop a surprise.

The only thing Emma knew for sure where Jake Morrow was concerned was that *she* loved him.

* * *

After a full morning of ranch chores and invoice paying and business, Jake finally told an excited Golden that yes, it was finally time to move all the nursery furniture they'd made into Emma's room. Making the chair and ottoman had been a first for Golden and he'd discovered he was a natural craftsman and carpenter and was now interested in starting his own side business. Jake loved watching Golden transform into a more confident young man.

Jake and CJ brought up the crib. Emma pointed to the spot she wanted it, against the wall near the window, and they positioned it. Grizzle reattached the mobile. Hank and Grizzle brought up the bookcase, and CJ and Golden brought up the rocker and ottoman. With the soft white walls and the colorful rug already in the room, the nursery looked complete. Redford had followed the crew and was now curled up on the rug, grooming his orange face with his paw.

"Can't believe a baby is going to be sleeping in that crib in just a few months," Grizzle said. "Makes me remember when my daughter was born. Most magical day of my life."

Emma smiled. "I can tell by all the love put into that mobile, Grizzle."

Grizzle smiled, and they all looked around the room. "We did good, guys."

"Thank you all so much from the bottom of my heart," Emma said. "I love the nursery. I love knowing all this was handmade by guardian angel cowboys."

Once the guys were sure that Emma liked where everything was placed, they headed downstairs to the kitchen to rustle up Italian sandwiches. Jake said he'd be down in a bit.

Emma sat in the rocker, leaning against the soft yellow back pad. "I went to see my dad after my shift at Hurley's. I tried to explain that even though I'm engaged, I wanted him to understand that I am self-sufficient and *could* raise my daughter on my own. I showed him my bank account records, talked about how independent and organized I am, and reminded him that I've been working full-time since I graduated from high school. He didn't hear a word I said."

"Because his issue isn't really with whether or not you *can* raise a baby by yourself, it's that he doesn't feel you *should*."

Emma sighed. She stood up and moved to the dresser and picked up the skinny, floppy-eared bunny that Grizzle had made with extra fabric from the mobile animals. "I know. I guess I thought if I could just get him to agree that I could do it, that of course I could do it and do it well, rule single-motherhood, I could slowly axe away at his old-fashioned notions."

"You'll be an amazing mother, Emma Hurley. I have no doubt about that."

She smiled and sat down on the edge of her bed, smoothing the bunny's long blue ears. "Thank you. My dad said the same thing. But then he added, 'well all that is a moot point to make now you have Jake.'"

You do have me, he wanted to shout from the roof. *Here I am.* But before he could say anything, her mouth dropped open and her hands flew to her belly.

He rushed over and knelt in front of her. "Emma? What's wrong?"

"Jake! The baby kicked! The baby kicked for the first time!"

Phew. For a second there he was worried something hurt or she needed help. "Can I?" he asked moving closer.

She nodded. She took his hand and placed it on her stomach. He couldn't feel the kick but he felt…something. Life. Energy. The future.

He tilted up her chin and kissed her, deepening it and she wrapped her arms around his neck. He ran his hand through her silky golden-brown hair. He could feel her lush breasts against his chest and he moved his hands around her back, to caress her face. He wanted her so badly.

"You're so beautiful, Emma," he said, and she kissed him so passionately she almost knocked the breath out of him.

He was about to rip off her T-shirt, dying to see what was underneath. Lace? Cotton? "I just realized that we're right in the middle of the nursery and any second, any of the guys could come walking through the door with the little extra decorations they've been making."

She looked at him and touched his face. She seemed to be debating something in her head. If this was a good idea or not.

It was. And wasn't.

Finally, she said, "Maybe we should close and lock the door, then."

Hot damn. *Yes*. It was a good and bad idea, but it was clear they both wanted each other. He got up long enough to lock the door, then was back on the bed where he lay Emma down against the blanket. He leaned up and slid the pale blue T-shirt over her head, lifting her pretty hair. The bra was white and lacy and so sexy he almost exploded on the spot.

But they'd make love and then what?

He knew what. He was balanced on a ledge right now, fine with how things were. The fake engagement. Everything had its place. They had an understanding. But the moment they had sex, made love, entwined their bodies, Jake would fall so hard that everything would topple. Literally and figuratively speaking. And there was too much at stake.

Like Emma's family farm.

Like his own self-preservation.

The more he thought about it, the more the faintly blinking yellow light in his brain turned into a bucket of cold water pouring on his head, down his jeans, dousing him in the face. Oh hell.

He ran his fingers through her silky golden-brown hair. "Emma, once we have sex, everything could change. I think we need to talk about that."

She bolted up and put her T-shirt back on. "You think I'm going to demand you marry me in the morning?" She glared at him. "Jake, you really are turning into Hank." With that, she got up and marched out, despite the fact that it was her bedroom they were in.

Redford gave Jake a dirty look and padded after Emma.

"I'm going to *want* to demand you marry me in the morning," he whispered to absolutely no one. But he had to get it through his thick skull—that wasn't what Emma wanted.

He had to let her go.

Chapter Eleven

Yes, Jake was avoiding Emma this morning. He'd gotten up earlier than usual, four fifteen, and grabbed a hard-boiled egg and a muffin and made himself coffee in a thermos, then headed out to the barn. At five, he heard Golden, Grizzle and Hank shuffling past on their way to the house for breakfast.

He moved farther into the barn to check on their littlest newborn goat, a weakling who the crew was taking turns watching and feeding. The sweet little white kid hungrily took the bottle Jake offered of its mother's milk. Every day the little guy was more able to stand firm on its spindly legs.

"You're Emma's favorite," he said to the kid. "I know she comes to feed you right after breakfast, but I was here so you're stuck with me." The little goat slurped away. He hoped Emma wouldn't mind too much that he'd fed the baby goat. "Soon I'll be feeding our baby with a bottle," Jake said. Out of the clear blue sky.

He froze. Our baby. Our baby? When had Emma's baby become *our baby*?

Since he was right there when little Violet had kicked for the first time and he'd felt the baby's energy right through Emma's belly. In that moment, Jake had understood—or thought he did, anyway—what it mean to feel like a father.

He felt like Baby Violet's father.

He wondered what Emma would think of that. Not much, very likely.

Unsettled with all these new and warring thoughts, Jake began mucking out stalls, the hard work good for his muscles and clearing his head. Before the crew had even emerged from the house from breakfast, he was out checking the far pastures. The ride and the cool morning air had done him good.

A couple of hours later, when Jake had just put Midnight back in his stall and threw some fresh hay, he heard a car pulling up in the drive. He brushed the hay bits from his jeans and headed outside. Who was this? Not Fern—she always drove her pickup. Not Michelle. Her car was white. As he got closer to the black SUV he saw it couldn't be Katie or Stella, given how petite they were and how big the person behind the wheel was. But whoever it was hadn't gotten out.

Jake stopped for a moment. The SUV had pulled over by the goat pasture. The driver sat there for a few moments, looking around. Then finally he opened the door.

A dark-haired man stepped out, no one Jake had

seen before. He was head to toe in black, including black cowboy boots. But this guy was no cowboy. Early thirties, Jake figured, tall, as tall as Jake, and easily as muscular, with the kind of sunglasses state troopers wore. He looked serious.

"I'm looking for Jake Morrow," the man said. He seemed to be staring intently at Jake, though Jake couldn't be sure because of the sunglasses.

"You found him," Jake said, extending his hand. "How can I help you?"

The man shook Jake's hand and cleared this throat. Then he took off his sunglasses. Green eyes, like Jake's, stared at him. "My name is Colt Asher."

Asher.

Jake almost gasped. "You're my— We're—"

"Twin brothers," Colt finished.

Jake wasn't often speechless. He was now. He gave himself a moment to think. "But how—"

Just then CJ tore out of the barn on Merlin, riding way too fast. From the brief glimpse on CJ's face, it was clear he was upset about something. He must have overheard Colt Asher introduce himself—and clearly remembered the name Asher from the index card on the adoption paperwork he'd found in his father's trunk.

"I received an email from CJ Morrow," Colt said.

Wait, what? He must have heard wrong. "CJ sent you an email?"

Colt nodded and handed over two sheets of paper. "Here. See for yourself."

What the hell? How had CJ found Jake's twin brother? And he'd sent him an email? Jake stared at the pages in Colt's hand. From: CJ's email address. To: Colt Asher's.

"Let's go inside the house," Jake said, the letter burning up his hand.

Colt nodded and followed him to the door. With every one of his nerve endings on fire, the cool interior was a relief. Jake led the way to the living room and gestured for Colt to sit where he liked. Jake sat across from him on the sofa.

"Can I get you something to drink? Iced tea? Coffee?"

"Actually, I'd love some coffee. Black and sweet."

Jake nodded and headed into the kitchen. He was grateful for the opportunity to step away for a moment, to let this sink in. His twin brother was in the living room.

Because CJ had emailed him.

Jake poured two mugs of coffee from the almost full pot, which meant it was fresh, added sugar for Colt and cream and sugar for himself. They didn't take their coffee the same way. First point of comparison that had come up.

Jake shook his head. He must be losing his mind. He was thinking about coffee habits? Who cared!

His twin brother, who he hadn't known existed until five years ago, was sitting in his living room. Looking an awful lot like Jake himself. The height, the physicality, the hair, the eyes.

He could barely wrap his mind around the fact that the guy was here, in his home, after all these years of Jake wondering about him, hoping to find him someday. He was here. In the flesh.

Because CJ had tracked him down. Jake supposed

between having the surname of the adoptive family and a Texas city, CJ had been able to find the right guy. From the looks of Colt Asher, Jake had no doubt CJ *had*.

Jake carried the two mugs back into the living room and handed one to Colt. The man nodded and took a sip. Jake sat back on the sofa and picked up the letter.

"We sure do look alike," Jake said. Anyone looking at them together would take them for brothers. They weren't anywhere close to identical, but the similarities were startling.

Colt nodded. "It's almost hard to look at you. When I first got the letter, I had to let it sink in at all that I had a twin brother. I've always known I was adopted. But I had no idea you existed."

That was one of the questions that had kept Jake up at night the past five years. Had his twin known? Or had he been in the dark like Jake most of his life? "I didn't know about you until five years ago. When I found out, from a notation on some paperwork concerning my adoption, I wrote the adoption agency to seek out our birth mother, thinking that would lead me to you. But then some things came up. I didn't actually connect with our birth mother until just a couple of months ago."

"You've met?" Colt asked, sipping his coffee.

Jake nodded, struck by how little Colt Asher gave away with his expression. He wouldn't be surprised to hear he was a poker player. Or a cop. "She lives right here in town. CJ and I are starting over here."

Colt seemed to let that sink in for a bit. "Speaking of CJ…why don't you read the email he sent me?"

Jake took a slug of his coffee and opened the envelope. He pulled out two pieces of white paper.

Dear Colt Asher,
My name is CJ Morrow. I'm writing because I recently found information in my late parents' belongings that say you are the twin of my brother, Jake Morrow. You and Jake were adopted by different families in Texas. Jake got stuck with me as a brother, and I'm ashamed to say that I haven't been living up to that title. Five years ago, when he found out you existed, he wanted to search for you, but I was seventeen then and we'd just lost our parents and I was afraid I'd lose him to you. How could a snot-nose kid like me compare to a biological brother, let alone a twin? For me, he quit the search. Lately, it's been consuming him—the idea of finding you, meeting you, just knowing something about you. But I stood in his way, and he cares too much about me and my stupid, selfish feelings to go ahead. So I'm getting out of his way and sending this for him. He's the best brother you'd ever hope for. Trust me, I know.
—CJ Morrow
Full Circle Ranch
Blue Gulch, Texas

"Wow," Jake said, so touched he couldn't say more for a minute.

Colt smiled. "That was my exact reaction. I can't stay long. I'm on a mission in this area, actually, so I was able to stop in for a few minutes."

"A mission?" Jake repeated.

"I'm an FBI special agent," Colt said. "I work out of Houston. I'm on a crazy case right now."

FBI agent. Of all the professions Jake had wondered about, from astronaut to author to doctor, he'd never thought federal agent.

Colt stood. "Unfortunately I have to go. But there was no way I could pass by Blue Gulch and not stop in. Once this case is over, I'd like to come back and maybe we can get to know each other."

Jake smiled. "I'd like that. And so would Sarah Mack—she's our birth mother."

"Sarah Mack." Colt nodded and turned to head toward the door. "I'll be back when I'm able. It might be several months, closer to November. Please thank your brother for writing that email."

"I will," Jake said. He walked Colt out to his car. "This might sound crazy but I feel…changed somehow by meeting you."

"I know exactly what you mean," Colt said, then put his sunglasses back on and got inside the car.

He watched Colt Asher's car disappear up the drive. His legs felt like they might give way so he leaned against the post. Colt Asher. His twin brother.

And CJ had found him for Jake. He still couldn't get over that. Or the beautiful email CJ had sent.

His cell phone rang. His foreman.

"Jake, Hank here. You need to come fast. Up by the far pasture. CJ's had an accident. It's bad."

Oh hell.

CJ was unconscious and had a broken leg, but the doctor has assured Jake he'd be fine. The waiting room was crowded with those who were waiting on word. The Full Circle crew. Emma. Stella.

He let Stella know that he was sure CJ would want her by his bedside and she tearfully raced in, her long, dark ponytail whipping behind her. The crew wanted to stay put until CJ woke up but had worked out a schedule so that two of them would take care of the necessities at the Full Circle for a couple hours while two stayed at the hospital. Hank and Golden had gone back to the ranch. Grizzle was sitting on one of the padded chairs in the waiting room, trying to avoid staring at the family of three sitting across from him, their eyes hollow and red-rimmed. A husband, around sixty or so, and two grown children, well into their thirties. A wife and mother in her early sixties, in a terrible car accident.

The doctor came out. He spoke quietly to the family.

"She's going to make it?" the husband repeated, barely able to speak.

"She'll need a lot of recuperation time," the doctor said, "but yes. You can see her when she wakes up."

The family burst into tears and latched on to one another with fierce grips.

"They're lucky," Grizzle whispered.

"They are," Emma said. "I guess when we lose people we love, we have to hold our memories even closer. That's how I keep my mother with me. I think about her, I know how she'd feel about this or that in my life and sometimes I even make decisions based on her advice. Is that crazy?"

"Not at all," Jake said. "My parents have been gone for five years and I can hear my dad's voice clear as a bell in my head sometimes. 'Now, Jake,' he'd say. And I know just what he'd tell me about any given situation." He smiled, the thought of his father very welcome in the midst of CJ lying in that hospital bed.

Grizzle didn't say anything. But then he leaned forward and said, "You want to know a secret?"

Emma nodded.

"It's like that for me too," Grizzle said, his voice a whisper. "And you want to know what my wife says about the way I keep my hair and beard? She thinks I'm a danged fool. 'Cut that hair! Trim that beard! And for God's sake, Harrison, put on a blasted suit for your date to meet Michelle's kin.'"

Jake saw tears glistening in Emma's eyes. "Grizzle, your name is Harrison? That's a great name."

"Well, of course my wife called me Harrison. Michelle always asks what my real name is but I tell her it's Grizzle."

"So you know your wife would like you to spiff up some and date Michelle?" Emma asked. "I didn't know that."

"She wants me to be happy," Grizzle said. He frowned, his face almost crumpling. "I'm the one… holding myself back."

"I could use a haircut," Jake said, running a hand through his thick, dark hair. "Maybe the both of us could go to the barbershop when Hank and Golden come back. "Look our Sunday best for CJ when he wakes up."

"Yeah," Grizzle said with a firm nod. "Yeah. Let's do that."

Jake wanted to hug the man but he settled for placing a hand on Grizzle's shoulder. "I'm gonna go get some coffee from the hospital cafeteria. Anyone want?"

"I'd love some decaf," Emma said.

"You two go ahead," Grizzle said. "I'll wait here for the guys. Bring me back a seltzer."

Jake nodded. "Will do."

He and Emma walked down the hall to the small cafeteria. A minute ago he'd been holding it together, but suddenly his chest felt like it was about to explode.

"What happened to CJ was my fault," he said and froze. He'd been so dumbstruck by meeting his twin that he hadn't even stopped to think about why CJ had been riding so fast and recklessly. Until he'd said the words, Jake hadn't realized how true it was.

Emma froze in the doorway. "Your fault? What do you mean?"

He took her by the hand and led her away from the line of people. "My twin brother came to the house today. His name is Colt Asher. Turns out CJ tracked him down via the little information we had from my adoption papers. I guess CJ saw a photo online of Asher and was sure he had the right guy, then emailed him. What he wrote blew me away."

Surprise lit her eyes. "Wow, Jake. You met your twin? And CJ tracked him down for you?"

"I can barely process any of it myself. I think Colt showed me the email because he was equally moved by it. CJ talked about how he'd been selfish to hold me back from trying to find my twin."

"What's he like?"

"He's an FBI agent," Jake whispered. "Imagine that. And we look a lot alike. He seems like a good guy."

"Wow," Emma said again. "Wow, wow, wow."

"I know. I almost can't believe it really happened, that he came to the ranch,, that we talked for a few minutes in the living room. He had to leave—he's on a case, but he said he'd be back when he could come."

"Wait a sec—Jake, how was CJ's accident possibly your fault?"

Jake let out a deep breath. "When my twin arrived, CJ must have seen him and I guess it was just too much for him to handle or something. He tore out of the barn on Merlin. The horse got spooked by something and threw CJ."

"Like with what happened to Joshua," Emma said on a whisper.

"He's so damned lucky to be alive. I'm so damned lucky. If I'd lost him—" He turned away, choking on his own thoughts.

"Jake, what happened to Joshua wasn't your fault. And CJ's accident wasn't your fault. Sometimes, accidents just happen. You can't blame yourself. CJ wanted you to have your twin in your life. He set that in motion, Jake. Not you."

"Because he knew how badly I wanted it. He did it at his own expense."

Emma put her hand on his arm. "That's what love is, Jake. That's what people who love each other do."

He stepped back. "Well, now CJ is unconscious in a hospital." He shook his head and walked out of the cafeteria.

He wanted to turn back, wanted to hug Emma and tell her he just needed time to let this all sit. But he found himself keeping going, farther and farther away.

* * *

"Dumb snake," CJ said.

Jake shot out of the chair beside CJ's hospital bed and stood over his brother, whose eyes were now open. Relief that CJ had finally woken up hit him so hard he almost had to sit down again. CJ looked groggy—but he was very much alive.

"It reared its creepy head and big amber-colored eyes right in front of Merlin," CJ said. "Nervy slitherer."

Jake smiled. "I figured it was something like that." He closed his eyes for a second. "Jesus, CJ. If you'd been killed—"

CJ grinned, his blue eyes twinkling. "You'll never get rid of me. That's a promise."

"Good," Jake said.

CJ moved up a bit in the bed, adjusting the pillow. "So you met Colt Asher, huh?"

"Thanks to you, yeah. You surprised the hell out of me."

"Someone had to, since it looked like you weren't going to track him down yourself. I know you think you were doing it—not doing it—for me. But the more I thought about it, the more I realized you weren't tracking him down for a different reason."

Jake frowned. "Like what?"

"Scared of what you might find? What he might turn out to be? The unknown? You run a tight ship for a reason, Jake. You don't like surprises. You never have."

Jake dropped back down in the chair. "I'm supposed to be the wise older brother. Not you."

"Well, if it wasn't for you knocking some sense in

my head, I might have lost Stella. I'm gonna propose to her when the doc springs me."

Jake's eyes widened. "Whoa. I'm happy for you, CJ. You're young, you're both young, but when you've found the person you know you want to spend forever with, I don't see the point in waiting."

"Unless you're you," CJ said. "Then you just go along with a fake engagement."

"Huh? The engagement *is* fake. There's nothing real about it."

"Right, brother. That's why it's so damned obvious to everyone else that you and Emma are in love. And I'm also including the ones who know the engagement is temporary. God, even her father buys it. That's how clear it is."

Jake frowned again. "I take back what I said about you being wise."

CJ laughed. "Sometimes the one right in it is the last to know. Like I was. Now it's you."

Before Jake could tell CJ just how wrong he was about his and Emma's fake engagement, the nurse came in for the vitals check. She was thrilled to see CJ had woken and paged his doctor.

Everyone believed he and Emma were in love? Jake supposed he could understand where folks would get that idea. He had gone to Emma's ultrasound appointment with her and seemed transfixed by the images right out in public. That reaction wasn't fake. And he did spend Saturday night's dance glued to Emma's side and talking to her until they got into their spat and she left—which might give some the idea there was passion between them.

As the nurse took CJ's blood pressure, Jake felt his

own rising. How exactly did he feel about Emma Hurley? He cared about her, yes. He thought she was stunningly beautiful and sexy, yes. He loved being around her, talking to her, listening to her, and he admired her worldview and the way she wanted to be on her own, be her own woman, even though he had to point out that accepting help and friendship didn't make her any less self-sufficient. He thought about her all the time. Fantasized about her at night as he lay in bed. Even Redford, *his* cat, had tossed him over for Emma, and now he slept curled up on the edge of her bed.

So did he love her? Ever since he'd met her, he'd tried to keep the word from his head, from moving too close to the surface of his heart where he might be too aware of it. He'd tamped his feelings back down, the way he always had.

Danged kid brother was right. About a lot of things. Hell yes, he loved Emma Hurley.

But how he felt about her was beside the point when he knew that Emma didn't want a real relationship or a father for her child. And how could he fight for her when doing so meant proving to her that he wasn't listening to what she wanted?

Jake's heart might be heavy, but he knew he could lighten someone else's with his news. Instead of heading home from the hospital, he drove to Edmund Ford's mansion, where Sarah Mack, his birth mother, lived.

As he parked beside Sarah's little yellow VW Beetle in the driveway, relieved that she was home, he was very aware that Sarah Mack was the one other person in the world who felt as he did where his twin was concerned. The wondering, the uncertainty, the burning in his veins to know *something*. Sarah felt that too.

Jake rang the bell and waited. The door opened, and there was Sarah, holding what looked to be a blond wig.

"Jake! I'm so glad to see you. I heard about your brother's accident and sent flowers to his hospital room. I'm so glad he's on the mend and will be fine. You must have been worried sick."

"I was. And very guilty."

"Guilty?" she repeated. "Why?"

"It has to do with why I'm here."

Her expression concerned, Sarah took his hand and led him inside, shutting the door behind him. "Edmund isn't home—he'll be sorry to have missed you—but I'm glad we'll have some private time to talk. What happened, Jake?"

"Going blond?" He gestured at the wig.

Sarah glanced at her hand. "Oh—I almost forgot I was holding it. I was about to practice on a new style a client is interested in trying. Better to mess up the wig than this client's gorgeous hair, trust me." She put the wig on a table. "Come sit in the kitchen. I just made coffee."

He followed her into the huge kitchen. Edmund Ford's house was amazing. Jake's ranch was pretty big, but Jake would say this house was three times the size of his. Somehow, the place managed to be homey and cozy. Maybe Sarah's doing.

Once they were seated with coffee, Jake said, "A man came to the Full Circle today. I didn't recognize his car and when he stepped out, he was wearing sunglasses. The moment he took off the shades I noticed we had very similar green eyes. Like yours."

Sarah gasped. She covered her mouth with her hand. "Your twin."

"Yes. His name is Colt Asher. Sarah, he's an FBI agent. He's on a case right now and couldn't stay longer than five minutes, but he said he'd be back when he could, probably around November, and we'd talk then."

"Oh my God. Colt Asher. How on earth…?"

"Remember I told you that my brother CJ had always been uncomfortable about the idea of my having a twin brother? Well, we came across a surname and city—Houston—on some old paperwork concerning the adoption in my father's old trunks in the attic. I wasn't planning on doing anything with the information—not just yet, anyway—but it turns out that CJ went ahead and tracked down my twin and emailed him."

"Wow," Sarah said. "I can't believe it."

"Me, either. I still can't wrap my mind around it. And apparently, CJ also couldn't, despite being the one to find the guy and bring him to me. When CJ saw him arrive, he got overwhelmed with what it meant, what it might mean for my relationship with CJ, and he booked out on a gelding and got thrown."

"Oh, I see. Oh, Jake, I hope you know that wasn't your fault."

"Well, I feel better about the whole thing because CJ is going to be fine. He has a broken leg, but it could have been a lot worse. We talked some in the hospital. Everything's fine between us now."

"I'm glad to hear it. I'm very touched by the fact that he wrote that email."

"That goes double for me."

"What's he like—our Colt Asher?"

"I couldn't get too much of a sense of him," Jake said. "He's very much a secret agent. That I could tell. But he seemed like a good person. I let him know you live in town too and he seemed glad to hear that. He'll be back around November, he said."

"Full circle," Sarah said, reaching for Jake's hand. "Like your ranch."

His heart moved in his chest. "Full circle."

Chapter Twelve

The sight before Emma was so startling, so shocking, that Emma almost dropped the long loaf of garlic bread she'd just pulled from the oven.

Grizzle stood before her in a suit and tie, his crazy, wild hair neatly cut, his beard shaved completely. "Came to tell ya I won't be here for dinner. I've decided to go to Michelle's and show her the new me and invite her to Hurley's or maybe that fancy Italian place for a change."

"Grizzle, you look so handsome," Emma said, almost speechless. She couldn't stop staring.

"When the barber finished shaving off the beard, I thought I wouldn't recognize myself," Grizzle said. "But it turns out I do, actually more than ever, if that makes sense. I feel like myself again. Isn't that nuts?"

"I think I understand," she said. "I'd hug you, but

I have marinara sauce all over my apron and I don't want to get a drop on that nice suit."

"Pretty spiffy, huh?" he said, glancing down at his dark blue jacket and pants with a gray tie with tiny black horses on it.

"Pretty spiffy," she repeated, absolutely wowed.

"Thanks for everything you did for me, Emma," he said. "You and Jake. He really didn't need a haircut, but he got one anyway to be in the chair next to mine."

That was Jake, all right. "I didn't do a thing. It was all you," she said.

"I'd better go. See you at breakfast."

Emma couldn't stop smiling as she ladled the fragrant meatballs into the big serving bowls, then added spaghetti with Aunt Essie's delicious marinara sauce, well, her recipe, into another dish.

But when she brought everything into the dining room, only Jake was sitting at the table. As always, she was struck by how incredibly handsome he was, how drawn she was to him. In her fantasy, they would have dinner by candlelight, their arms entwined as they fed each other spaghetti, unromantic as meatballs and spaghetti might be.

She liked his haircut. Short, but still slightly ruffled and impossibly sexy.

"Just you and me tonight," he said, raising his beer glass at her.

"I hope you're hungry, then. I made a ton of meatballs. I know Hank loves his meatballs so I went a little overboard. He'll have them tomorrow for lunch, I'm sure." She could ramble on and on. Why was Jake making her so nervous? Because they were alone? Because she was in love?

"I barely ate today because I was so worried about CJ. Now that I know he's awake and will be coming home tomorrow, I'm starving."

She smiled. "I'm so glad he's going to be fine. Where are the guys?"

Jake served himself a heaping portion of spaghetti and added three meatballs on top. "Turns out Hank is on a date with Fern. Golden is out with Katie at a lecture. CJ won't be home till tomorrow. And Grizzle said he was going to stop in to show you his transformation before going to Michelle's."

"I was speechless. And my heart almost burst. He's come to mean so much to me. All the cowboys have."

He took a sip of his beer. "You know, that first day you came here, I asked if you'd give the guys some tips on dealing with women and relationships, and suddenly, they're *all* transformed. Am I paying you enough?"

She grinned. "And then some." But she could feel her smile begin to fade as she looked at the ring on her finger, her mother's beautiful diamond in the gold band.

Jake's words in the hospital came back to her— about why CJ had tracked down Jake's twin. *Because he knew how badly I wanted it. He did it at his own expense.*

She stared at the ring and recalled her own response. *That's what love is, Jake. That's what people who love each other do.*

The proposal. The agreement to the fake engagement. Coming to her ultrasound appointment. The nursery furniture.

The kisses, few and far between, but kisses, none-theless.

Could her aunt Essie have been right, after all? Did Jake Morrow love her?

Jake then took a piece of garlic bread. "I'm sorry I walked away from you in the hospital. I was pretty overwhelmed. But CJ and I had a good talk. He's going to propose to Stella."

"Wow!" Emma said. "That's great. "And I know you must be very relieved that he's going to be okay."

Jake twirled spaghetti on his fork. "I am. I talked to CJ about why he sent the letter. He said he did it because he knew how much I wanted to meet my twin but that he also knew I might never actually go through with it. Out of fear of the unknown. I wonder if he's right about that."

"When you found out you had a twin you never knew existed, you wrote a letter to your birth mother to be placed in your adoption file," she pointed out.

He nodded. "That's true. But that was five years ago and I remember being relieved when she didn't respond until very recently. He said I didn't like surprises and that's true. I guess I like knowing what's what."

Emma glanced at her handsome faux fiancé. This whole situation had to be so hard for him. "I guess you'll be relieved when we can call off the fake en-gagement, then," she said, feeling like a heel for fish-ing but unable to ask him outright how he felt.

"Of course I will," he said, breaking off a piece of garlic bread.

She waited for a "but." For more. For any additional words to follow, but he just gave her a tight smile and twirled spaghetti on his fork.

She felt her heart split in two. She knew he didn't love her. That all this time he was just being Jake Morrow, the ultimate cowboy riding to her rescue at his own expense.

She pushed around a meatball on her plate, her appetite gone. "I'm going to tell my dad the truth."

Jake stared at her. "What? He'll sell the farm."

She put down her fork. "I've been doing a lot of thinking. About truth and doing what's right even when it hurts like hell. You proposed to me because you thought it was the right thing to do under the circumstances, despite *everything*. CJ wrote that email to your twin even though it scared him to death. If I want to live by my rules and stand on my own two feet, I need to let my mother's farm go. I need to practice what I preach."

"But, Emma, you don't have to stand alone. I—"

He didn't finish his sentence. He took a slug of his beer. But she had no doubt about what he was about to say. That she had him. That she didn't have to be a lone wolf.

"I have to stand up for living honestly," she said. "That's always been my whole point. To live on my own terms. But I'm not doing that. I used to think it was about not letting my father control me and tell me how to live my life. But I've come to realize, thanks to you and the crew, that there's a difference between controlling someone and offering support or a shoulder or a hand. You're the latter, Jake. And to be truthful, I've liked having a strong shoulder. I've liked having good friends. But it's time to tell the truth."

She ran out before he could try to stop her.

* * *

Jake sat on the porch in the waning light, Redford on his lap. Emma had left only five minutes ago and it felt like an hour. Two hours. If he took CJ's little speedracer, he could easily catch up to her on the main road. She'd get out of her car. He'd get out of his. He'd run to her and tell her not to confess the truth to her father because he wanted their engagement to be real. He wanted to propose for real, slip that ring off her finger and put it back on for real. He wanted to marry her. Not to save the farm.

Because he loved her.

He knew with absolute clarity, and yet he remained seated in the chair. When you loved someone, you had to let her go if that's what she wanted, and that was what Emma wanted.

Even if you broke your heart doing it.

Emma walked through the apple orchard, saying goodbye, apologizing to her mother for not being able to keep the farm in the family, and holding back tears that kept threatening. She was meeting her father in the house in five minutes to "talk about something" important, and she needed to be clear-eyed.

She stood surveying the back of the house. There was the patio where her mother had brought out just about every one of Emma's birthday cakes on the table. There was the tire swing hanging from the old oak. There was the spot where her first boyfriend had broken her heart by telling her he didn't like her, after all, and was now dating someone with bigger boobs. But mostly she recalled walking through these fields with not just her mother but her father, the three of them together. This was their home. Her father had loved her mother—Emma believed that more than she believed anything.

So how could he want to sell her beloved homestead just to get his way? Emma still couldn't wrap her mind around that.

She glanced at her cell phone for the time. She had to go in and face the music, face the truth. *You can't have everything*, she chanted to herself. *You have your baby-to-be. You have your future. But you don't have Jake and you won't have this farm.* A sob rose up in her throat and she forced it back.

You won't have a fake engagement, she reminded herself, squaring her shoulder and lifting her chin. It was fake. Fake, fake, fake.

Feeling better, Emma headed in through the back door. Her father was in the kitchen, putting his key ring into the white marble dish on the counter and fixing himself a drink.

Emma poured herself a cranberry juice and seltzer and went into the living room and sat down. Above the fireplace was an oil painting of the Hurleys—Reginald, Violet and Emma. Again, a sadness gripped her but she moved to a chair that didn't face the painting.

"What was so hellfire important?" her father asked, sitting down with his drink. He stirred the lime around the short glass and Emma was transfixed by it, mentally grabbing on to anything to stall. "Please tell me everything is okay with the baby."

She appreciated the concern in his voice. "Yes, the baby is fine, Dad." She cleared her throat. "I need to be honest with you about something."

Reginald Hurley snapped his gaze to her. He looked as though he was bracing himself for the worst.

Emma put down her drink on the coffee table, took a breath, and said, "About this." She held up her left hand, where her mother's diamond ring gleamed. She slid it off her finger and put it on the table. Suddenly she felt bereft, as though she'd lost something very dear and special. But how could that be when she and Jake were never engaged for real?

"What is this?" her father asked, his blue eyes worried. "What's going on? You got into a fight?"

"Dad—"

"Emma, all couples argue. And all couples work it out. You and Jake are meant to be together. I know that more than I know anything."

Tears pricked Emma's eyes. "Dad, Jake and I—"

"I'll tell you a little family secret," Reginald said. "You probably won't believe this, but your mother broke up with me after we were engaged. She gave me the ring back and everything. She told me I was too controlling and she would not live her life under my thumb."

Emma gasped. "Mom never told me that."

Reginald Hurley sipped his drink. "I'm not surprised. Violet was pretty private."

"Well, I know you did get married, so what happened?"

Her father glanced up at the family painting, and she knew he was looking specifically at Violet Hurley. Then he looked back at Emma. "I told her that the reason I tried so hard to make everything perfect and keep things in tidy boxes, as she called it, was because I was afraid of everything toppling over. I believe if you do things right, the first time, then you've got a fighting chance."

"That was enough to make her take back the ring?" Emma asked. It couldn't possibly be.

"No. She made me make a promise. That if she was going to marry a man as bossy as I am, that we would have discussions of everything we disagreed on and neither of our votes would cancel something out. If I disagreed with someone she wanted to do or buy, I would have to get over it. And vice versa."

Emma raised an eyebrow. She tried to think back on ever overhearing her parents' disagreements over the years and how they'd resolved things. Her mother had gone on a girls' weekend every year with her best friends from high school and Reginald Hurley didn't like it one bit, but off she'd gone, every year. And Violet Hurley couldn't stand that Reginald would spend a fortune on golf clubs every other year, but his collection constantly grew.

"I think you and Jake should just come to some sort of agreement," Reginald concluded. "Make some sort of pact about how you'll compromise. That's the couples' way."

"We did, Dad. That's the problem." She closed her eyes for a moment, bracing herself for what she was about to say. The truth. "Jake and I were never really planning to marry. He was my fake fiancé so that you wouldn't sell the farm."

Her father stood up, anger shooting from his blue eyes. "Of all the underhanded—"

Oh hell, as Jake would say. She felt awful, no matter how necessary she'd thought her lie had been. "I thought if I could just convince you that I'm capable, that I can manage on my own, you wouldn't sell Mom's farm." Tears streamed down her cheeks.

She really had believed she could do it. That her father would love her more than he cared about propriety. That he didn't love her more than that hurt like hell.

Reginald Hurley crossed his arms over his chest and continued to glare at her.

She might as well tell him the whole truth, she thought, her heart clenching. "And all I managed to do is fall deeply in love with my fake fiancé. I didn't convince you of anything. And now I'm going to lose everything I love."

She wondered what this would mean for her job. Could she bear working at the Full Circle? Living under the same roof with a man who didn't return her feelings?

"Emma, I don't think I've ever been so disappointed," her father said, putting down his glass. He shook his head and turned away.

"I understand that," she said, trying to blink back her tears. "But at least I'm not lying anymore. I love you, Dad, even if you *are* controlling and want things your way. I wish we could have worked out a system like you and Mom had, that both our feelings count. But I suppose in your eyes I'll always be your child and not your equal."

Reginald Hurley stared at her, his eyes narrowing.

She stood up and sucked in a breath. "In some ways I certainly do take after you with how stubborn I am. I won't be marrying Jake Morrow. Or anyone."

With one last look at the ring on the table, Emma ran out.

* * *

Emma spent the next hour driving around town, her stomach in knots, her head a jumble of thoughts. She'd lied to her father and he was furious. He was going to sell the farm.

For a while there, before she'd confessed that the engagement was a sham, she'd thought her father was remembering their life as a family and the compromises—good compromises—he'd made to have a happy life with his wife. She'd felt a glimmer of hope that he'd include her in that compromise, that he knew he couldn't have a "my way or the highway" mentality and expect her to hop to it.

Emma, I've never been so disappointed...

Now, as she looked out on the landmarks and shops and restaurants that had been such a huge part of her life for the past twenty-six years, she couldn't imagine Oak Creek not being part of her world. But how could Oak Creek feel like her hometown once the farm was sold? How could she come back here?

All this strife and stress couldn't be good for Baby Violet. She needed to get her head together. Maybe a decaf iced latte with extra whip cream would help. She parked in front of the coffee shop and when she got out of her car, she heard someone call her name.

Emma turned and there was her friend Olivia Mack with her aunt Sarah Mack. Olivia was a sight for a sore heart. Emma adored Olivia, who'd been so kind to her in her early days in Blue Gulch. Olivia trained her in cooking food for the Hurley's Homestyle Kitchen food truck. But then Emma realized with a start that Sarah Mack was Jake's birth mother. And Emma wasn't wearing her engagement ring.

Sarah's eyes beelined right to Emma's left hand. But clearly, thoman was too polite to say anything because she didn't ask why she wasn't wearing her ring or if everything was all right.

"Emma," Olivia said, her warm brown eyes thoughtful, "I hope you don't mind me saying so, but you look very upset. If you'd like to sit down and talk, we're good listeners."

Emma almost burst into tears. All she could do was nod. Sarah put her arm around Emma and led the way inside the coffee shop.

With their coffee drinks and treats in hand, they found a table in the back, away from eavesdroppers. Oak Creek was a small town and Emma certainly wouldn't want anything she said to be overheard.

"I guess you might have noticed that I'm not wearing my engagement ring," Emma said, squeezing her eyes shut for a second. "I'm just going to tell you the truth." She launched into the whole story, ending with what just happened at her dad's house.

"Oh wow, Emma," Olivia said. "I'm so sorry."

Sarah reached over and squeezed Emma's hand.

The support felt so good. She was so lucky she'd run into Olivia and Sarah. "The ring is sitting there on that coffee table in my father's house. When I want nothing more than for it to be on my finger for *real*. What a mess this turned out to be. At first, I didn't want to get married. Then I agreed to a fake engagement to save the farm. Then I fell in love with a fake fiancé who doesn't love me back. And then I had to be honest with my dad and give back the ring. I've lost the farm and I'm going to lose Jake too."

"Emma, does Jake know how you feel about him?" Sarah asked.

For a moment, Emma was struck by how much Jake looked like his birth mother. Though Jake had dark hair and Sarah's was auburn, they both had the same beautiful green eyes and strong, straight nose.

"No. How could I tell him? Jake is a stand-up guy. He stepped up to save my mother's house for me. How could I lay on him that I love him and do want a life with him when that's not what he signed up for? He was so clear in the beginning that he didn't want a relationship. And anyway, he said this morning at breakfast that he'd be relieved when the whole fake engagement thing came to an end."

Olivia broke off a piece of peanut butter brownie. "Maybe because, as it was for you, that got flipped on its head. Maybe he developed strong feelings for you too. And having to be in a fake relationship with someone you care about is hard on the heart, mind and soul."

Hope blossomed and Emma latched on to it. She knew that Olivia was the daughter of a popular fortune-teller who'd passed away last winter. Sometimes, just from listening to Olivia talk or watching the effect her po'boys and cannoli had on her customers at the food truck, Emma got the sense that Olivia had special abilities of her own. The pretty young woman just seemed to know things—and her food seemed to lift spirits and moods. Or maybe Emma was crazy and seeing what wasn't there. She just knew the conviction in Olivia's voice came from a place Emma could believe in. That helped.

But still. "So I just walk up to him and say, 'Hey

Jake, is there any chance that you might love me? Because I love you and if you love me, let's get that out in the open.'"

Sarah laughed. "Sounds a little nutty, but yes. Or, since you're being very brave and honest with yourself and your father, just tell Jake how *you* feel. And see what happens."

Tell Jake how she felt? And have to watch his handsome face as he said the words that would break her heart in a million pieces. *Emma, I'm sorry, but I don't feel that way. I proposed to help you out. I went along with the fake engagement to help you out. But now that you went and told your dad the truth, we're kind of done here.*

Okay, she knew he wouldn't say that, exactly. But she knew she'd get exactly what she'd said she always wanted: to be on her own.

What was that old adage about being careful what you wished for?

"That goes for your dad too, Emma," Olivia said. "How can he sell your family home? You said he was talking about your mom earlier. Maybe now that he's had some time to think about how far you went to try to save the house, he'll soften a bit."

"I don't know. He was very upset. But I can give it one last try."

Sarah nodded. "One thing I've learned is that you always have to give it that last try. Sometimes that's when everything comes together."

Emma took a deep breath and another sip of her decaf latte. "Yes. One last try. I'll plead my case. I'm going to tell my dad I'm sorry for lying to him, but that the house and farm mean so much to me that I thought I had to play this crazy game. I'll state my case that I'm a strong, self-sufficient woman who can and will be a good mother on my own. And if he still decides to sell, well, I'll know I tried."

"And Jake?" Olivia asked, her brown eyes prodding.

How could she not try? Was she willing to walk away from the man she loved just like that? No.

"And Jake. One last try. I'm going to tell him how I feel. If he says, 'Sorry, it was all for show, all for the fake engagement,' at least I'll know I told him, that I put myself out there. That's what brave, strong self-sufficient women do, right?"

"Yes," Sarah said. "It's the only thing any of us can do. We can just be honest with ourselves and others and put the truth out there."

"Thank you both so much for talking this through with me," Emma said. "I hope Jake won't be upset that I spilled the beans to you, particularly, Sarah. I know he'd have preferred to tell you himself."

"Well, we're friends, Emma," Sarah said. "And friends help each other when it's needed. So no worries. I'm sure Jake will understand."

Emma smiled, hugged Olivia and Sarah and then hurried to her car. She wanted to talk to her father as soon as possible.

As she drove to the house, she wondered if her dad would even listen to her. Or see her. He was angry— clearly. But surely he'd understand why she'd gone to such lengths to keep the house in the family.

There was no way Reginald Hurley could want to sell his late wife's homestead and legacy. Especially with a grandchild on the way.

Of course. Now that her dad had had some time to cool down, they would talk and try to reach some kind of common ground.

As Emma approached her family home, her heart slowed and the blood drained from her face. She pulled over, her stomach lurching.

No. No, no, no.

There was a for-sale sign in the front yard.

Chapter Thirteen

Jake had been stalking around the house and pastures for the past two hours waiting for Emma to come home. Had she talked to her dad? What the hell had he said? Had they made up?

Jake stopped pacing by the front door and looked out the windows at the darkening sky. Still no Emma. She and her father must have had a good talk, then. Otherwise, she would have been home in five minutes, a wreck about her dad planning to go through with his threat to sell the farm.

He heard a car coming down the drive and went outside. Emma. He stood on the porch with Redford at his shin, waiting for her to get out of the car, but she didn't. She was just sitting there. Not moving.

Oh hell.

He went over and opened the door. She was sobbing, her shoulders shaking. He reached in and scooped her into his arms and she let him, wrapping her own arms around his neck. He shut the car door with his foot and carried Emma in the house and upstairs to her room.

Once inside he lay her down on the bed and she covered her face with her hands.

"There's a for-sale sign on the front lawn of my family home," she said through ragged breaths. "I don't know what hurts more—that he'd actually sell the place or that he doesn't care how much it kills me."

"Oh hell," he said for the millionth time that day. "I'm sorry, Emma. I really didn't think he'd make good on his threat."

She closed her eyes and he lay down beside her, lifting her up a bit so that her head rested on his chest. He put his arms around her and just held her.

The doorbell rang, the clang breaking the stillness in the room.

"No idea who that could be," Jake said. "I'd hate to ignore it in case it's someone needing help." He got up and went to the window and pushed aside the curtain. "Em—doesn't your dad have a fancy silver SUV?"

"Yes," she said, confusion crossing her features. "Is it my dad?" She walked over to the window. "That's his car. I guess he's here to tell me about the house being for sale. A neighbor probably already made him an offer. The Sanders family have wanted the farm for ages." Her face crumpled but she lifted her chin.

The doorbell rang again. "Let's go," Jake said, taking her hand. "Together."

The bell rang again just as Jake opened the door.

Reginald Hurley stood there, imposing as usual. He nodded at Jake and turned his attention to Emma.

Hurley cleared his throat, and then he reached into his jacket pocket for a piece of paper that he unfolded. A flyer of some kind. "Emma, I thought you might be interested in this property for sale. I'll sell it to you for one dollar."

Emma moved closer and looked at the flyer. It was a picture of her family home. Her mother's farm. All the pertinent information was listed below.

Emma's mouth dropped open. "Wait. What?"

"Reginald, why don't you come in?" Jake said, opening the door wider. The man stepped in. Jake closed the door behind him, and then they all went into the living room.

Reginald sat down on the sofa. "I've been thinking about what I said when you were over earlier. About the compromises your mother had me make. They were tough on me, I don't have to tell you that."

Emma managed a smile. "I know, Dad."

"I had a plan for you, Emma. High school valedictorian. A good college, but close enough to commute. A good job in a dependable industry. Then marriage. Starting a family. Staying at home with your children. A good life." He leaned back against the sofa.

"So far, none of that has happened," she said.

Reginald almost snorted. "I know. And when you left earlier, I sat there staring at the engagement ring I gave your mother. The one built on compromise. When I told you weeks ago that your mother would turn over in her grave to see you pregnant and alone and working for room and board as a cook on a ranch,

I was wrong. Your mother would turn over in her grave to know how I've treated you."

Jake could see Emma blinking back tears. Hell, even he wanted to rush over to Reginald Hurley and hug the man.

"Oh, Dad," Emma said.

"I don't like it, Emma. Not one bit. You being pregnant and on your own. But it's your life and my job as your father is to be there for you. Not turn my back." His face tightened and now his own eyes glistened with tears. "I will never turn my back on you again, Emma. Never."

Emma stood up and rushed over to her father, flinging herelf into his arms. They hugged for a good minute.

"I love you, Dad."

"I love you, Emma. With all my heart. But about the house. It's just too darn big for me at this point. I want to downsize to a condo in town. The house is your legacy and belongs to you." He reached into his pocket and pulled something out. Jake peered closer. The ring—her mother's diamond that Jake had slid on Emma's finger. His chest tightened. "Emma, I want you to have this. One day, if you want to marry, you'll have it."

That earned Reginald Hurley another hug.

The man stood, looking very much at peace with himself. "I'd better get going. I'll have the paperwork drawn up for the sale. Get that dollar ready. See you soon, Emma?"

She smiled. "Very soon, Dad. Can you come in for lunch at Hurley's on Saturday? We can have the special after my shift. It's your favorite that you never let yourself have. Chicken-fried steak and garlic mashed potatoes."

"It's a date," Reginald said. He glanced at Jake. "I'd like it if you joined us, Jake. I'd love to hear about the ranch and what it takes to start up a place like this. I always liked the idea of investing in therapeutic horses for kids and adults. I had a brother who benefited from that as a kid."

Jake extended his hand. "I'd love to talk more about that."

Emma was beaming. She hugged her dad goodbye again and they walked Reginald out to his car. Both watched the silver SUV drive away.

"Wow," Emma said. "I'm so dumbstruck with happiness I can't even speak."

"I'm very happy for you, Emma. And relieved." He took her hand and led the way into the living room. They both sat down on the sofa, turned to face each other.

"I ran into your birth mother and her niece in Oak Creek a few hours ago. I was distraught over the talk with my dad and I ended up telling them everything. I hope that's okay with you, Jake. I mean, I told Sarah that the engagement wasn't real."

"It's fine," he said. "Don't give that another thought."

"I'll never forget what you did for me," she said. "Hiring me in the first place. Proposing. The fake engagement. Thank you."

"I'd do it all again," he said. His chest tightened up again. This was it. Where she said she would take it from here, be on her own.

"Your birth mother gave me some advice."

"Oh yeah?"

"She said everything was about trying. That you had to try, put yourself out there. Especially one last time."

Jake nodded. "Sarah's wise. I completely agree with that." *So stand up. Tell her how you feel. If she says, "sorry, I can't," at least you put it out there. At least she knows.*

He stood up.

She stood up.

"You first," she said, biting her lip.

He took both her hands. "Emma. Here's the thing. I might have proposed to you to help you save your family house. I might have agreed to be fake engaged for that same reason. But the times I kissed you, that was because I think you're the most beautiful woman I've ever seen. And because when I look at you, when I think about you, when I talk to you, when I kiss you, I feel like I'm home. I feel like I've found forever. I love you so much I can't breathe around you sometimes."

She gasped. "Jake."

"I know. You're flattered. You appreciate all that. You care about me. But you want to be on your own right now. I understand that. I respect your feelings." He turned away and walked to the window that looked out onto the goat pasture. He could see Goatby, that little devil, trying to butt the fence for another escape.

He almost smiled at the thought of Goatby escaping the pen that day Emma first arrived, he and CJ chasing after him. Coming home to dinner on the table.

His life changed, just like that.

Love had come. And now it was going.

He heard her walk over to him, felt her press herself against his back, her arms wrap around his waist.

He turned around and she looked up at him and kissed him, hard and passionately. "Okay, that wasn't what I expected."

"Jake Morrow, when I realized how deeply in love with you I am, I did get pretty scared. I tried to talk myself out of it. But some truths are just too big."

She loved him too. *Yes!*

He grinned and pulled her close, careful of her belly. "I know what you mean. I think I tried the same thing."

"I love you so much, Emma. Will you do me the honor of becoming my wife? For real."

"For real. Yes," she said and reached up and kissed him.

"Tell you what," he said. "I'm going to make us a very romantic little snack involving chocolate and strawberries. You call your dad—put the man out of his misery."

Emma laughed. She pulled her phone from her pocket and pressed in her father's number. "Dad? I have you on speaker. I thought you should be the first to know that I am really and truly—for real—engaged to marry Jake Morrow. I'm counting on you to walk me down the aisle this summer."

"I'm so happy for you, Emma," Reginald said, his voice breaking. "I knew there was something between you two!"

"Everybody did. We were the last to know. Well, we knew, but we both tried to hide from it. Turns out you can't hide from love that big."

"No, you can't. I tried with you and it hit me upside the head, didn't it?"

"Love you, Dad," she said. When she pocketed her phone, her heart was so full she thought it might burst glitter all over the living room floor.

Jake came back into the living room with a tray. Chocolate melted in a little fondue pot. Strawberries. And a bottle of apple cider with two wineglasses. "Shall we continue this engagement celebration upstairs in private?"

"What about him?" Emma said, gesturing at Redford, who sat staring at them.

"Just us," Jake said. "Sorry, Redford."

Emma laughed and walked beside her husband-to-be up the stairs, a brand-new family formed.

Epilogue

On a breathtaking June afternoon, with powdery white clouds in the brilliant blue sky, Jake stood at the altar under the linen canopy that the cowboys had made and which Fern, Stella, Michelle and Katie had woven through with white and pink roses.

The wedding march began and every head in every chair turned to watch the bride begin her walk down the aisle, her arm entwined with Reginald Hurley. The man looked very proud and happy. Jake's legs almost buckled at the sight of Emma, in a long, white satiny dress, a simple filmy veil over her face, walking toward him. Emma had told him that the dress was her "something borrowed" from her cousin Georgia, who had worn it to walk down the aisle while very noticeably pregnant too.

In just a few months, Jake would be a father. He

and this beautiful woman, who would in moments be his wife, would unite as a family and raise Baby Violet together. Lately, Jake had gone a little overboard in BabyCenter, buying little lavender-colored pajamas and soft blankets and teething toys. Everytime he came home with a bursting shopping bag, Emma would roll her eyes with a smile and ooh and ahh over the adorable items he'd bought. Emma had asked Jake what he thought about giving Violet the middle name of Smith, to honor Joshua Smith, and he thought that was a beautiful idea. Violet Smith Morrow, it was.

As he watched Emma step closer and closer to him, he could hardly believe how blessed he was.

Finally, she stood beside him. Her father lifted the veil and there was his stunning Emma, the woman he loved. When the minister pronounced them husband and wife and he kissed his bride, a surge of happiness shot through him.

The guests jumped up and clapped, CJ's wolf whistles the loudest of them all. As waiters carrying trays of champagne and hors d'oeuvres weaved through the crowd, Jake slow-danced with his brand-new wife, holding her close. Just a few feet away he saw CJ dipping his fiancée, Stella. Grizzle, still clean-shaven and wearing a "spiffy" blue suit, was twirling Michelle around. Hank and Fern were cheek to cheek. And Golden and Katie had their arms around each other's necks, staring into each other's eyes. It was anyone's guess who the next couple to say "I do" would be.

Off in the distance, a glint by a tree caught Jake's eyes. Someone, a man, was holding up a glass of champagne as if in toast. Was that… Colt Asher?

Jake swore it was. His twin brother stood in the

shadows, clearly still undercover or needing to keep himself hidden.

Jake blinked and like that, Colt Asher was gone. But he'd come. He'd come to witness this day and that meant a lot to Jake. Soon enough they'd be able to talk.

"I love you, Emma Hurley Morrow," Jake said, kissing his bride softly on the lips.

She looked into his eyes and kissed him. "I love you."

"Hey," he said, glancing just past her shoulder. "Is that your dad dancing with your great aunt Essie?"

Emma turned and gasped. "Wow. My dad has really changed. On the phone yesterday, I asked him to try and patch things up with Essie, that it was time for new beginnings. He gave me a humph, but said, 'we'll see,' which is always a good sign. And now here they are, not only speaking, but dancing!"

"Looks like your work here really is done," Jake said. "Me. Your dad. The crew."

Jake watched Emma turn to look at each of the men whose heart she helped turn around. Her smile was so breathtaking that Jake's heart clenched.

The five men of the Full Circle Ranch danced with their ladyloves, all graduates—with honors—of Emma's charm school for cowboys.

* * * * *

*Look for Colt Asher's story
in November 2017 as the
HURLEY'S HOMESTYLE KITCHEN
series continues!*

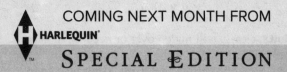

COMING NEXT MONTH FROM

HARLEQUIN®

SPECIAL EDITION

Available May 23, 2017

#2551 WILD WEST FORTUNE

The Fortunes of Texas: The Secret Fortunes • by Allison Leigh

Ariana Lamonte is making her name as a journalist by profiling the newly revealed Fortunes. When she finds three more hidden in middle-of-nowhere Texas, including the sexy rancher Jayden Fortune, she thinks she's hit the jackpot. Until she falls for him! Will this professional conflict of interest throw a wrench in their romance?

#2552 A CONARD COUNTY HOMECOMING

Conard County: The Next Generation • by Rachel Lee

Paraplegic war veteran Zane McLaren just wants to be left alone to deal with the demons his time in the army left behind. Fortunately, his service dog, Nell, has other ideas that include his pretty neighbor, Ashley Granger.

#2553 IN THE COWBOY'S ARMS

Thunder Mountain Brotherhood • by Vicki Lewis Thompson

Actor Matt Forrest has just landed his first big-budget role when scandal forces him to flee Hollywood for the Wyoming ranch he grew up on. His PR rep, Geena Lysander, hopes to throw a positive light on the situation, never expecting their cool, professional relationship to heat up into something more personal!

#2554 THE NEW GUY IN TOWN

The Bachelors of Blackwater Lake • by Teresa Southwick

Florist Faith Connelly has sworn off men, but sexy newcomer Sam Hart tempts her, even though both of them have painful pasts to look back on. Because he buys flowers from her, she knows he's a "two dates and you're out" kind of guy, so what's the harm in flirting a little? But when a wildfire forces Faith to take shelter with Sam, both of them confront the past in order for love to grow.

#2555 HONEYMOON MOUNTAIN BRIDE

Honeymoon Mountain • by Leanne Banks

When recently divorced Vivian Jackson and her sisters decide to take over their deceased father's hunting lodge, Vivian runs into her long-ago crush, Benjamin Hunter. He turned her down as a teen, but he's giving her more than a second look now. Their affair burns out of control, but it'll take more than heat to deal with Benjamin's secrets and Vivian's fear of failing at love again.

#2556 FALLING FOR THE RIGHT BROTHER

Saved by the Blog • by Kerri Carpenter

When Elle Owens returns to Bayside, she hopes everyone has forgotten the embarrassing incident that precipitated her flight from town ten years ago. They haven't, but Cam Dumont, her former crush's sexy older brother, doesn't care what anyone thinks—he's determined to win her over. Can Elle forget about the ubiquitous Bayside Blogger long enough to tell Cam how she truly feels about him?

SPECIAL EXCERPT FROM

H HARLEQUIN®
™

SPECIAL EDITION

*Zane McLaren just wants to be left alone to deal with
the demons his time in the army left behind. Fortunately,
his service dog, Nell, has other ideas—ideas that
include his pretty neighbor, Ashley Granger.*

Read on for a sneak preview of
CONARD COUNTY HOMECOMING,
the next book in New York Times
bestselling author **Rachel Lee's**
CONARD COUNTY: THE NEXT GENERATION
miniseries.

Things had certainly changed around here, he thought as
he drove back to his house. Even Maude, who had once
seemed as unchangeable as the mountains, had softened
up a bit.

A veterans' group meeting. He didn't remember if
there'd been one when he was in high school, but he
supposed he wouldn't have been interested. His thoughts
turned back to those years, and he realized he had some
assessing to do.

"Come in?" he asked Ashley as they parked in his
driveway.

She didn't hesitate, which relieved him. It meant he
hadn't done something to disturb her today. Yet. "Sure,"
she said and climbed out.

His own exit took a little longer, and Ashley was
waiting for him on the porch by the time he rolled up
the ramp.

Nell took a quick dash in the yard, then followed eagerly into the house. The dog was good at fitting in her business when she had the chance.

"Stay for a while," he asked Ashley. "I can offer you a soft drink if you'd like."

She held up her latte cup. "Still plenty here."

He rolled into the kitchen and up to the table, where he placed the box holding his extra meal. He didn't go into the living room much. Getting on and off the sofa was a pain, hardly worth the effort most of the time. He supposed he could hang a bar in there like he had over his bed so he could pull himself up and over, but he hadn't felt particularly motivated yet.

But then, almost before he knew what he was doing, he tugged on Ashley's hand until she slid into his lap.

"If I'm outta line, tell me," he said gruffly. "No social skills, like I said."

He watched one corner of her mouth curve upward. "I don't usually like to be manhandled. However, this time I think I'll make an exception. What brought this on?"

"You have any idea how long it's been since I had an attractive woman in my lap?" With those words he felt almost as if he had stripped his psyche bare. Had he gone over some new kind of cliff?

Don't miss
CONARD COUNTY HOMECOMING
by Rachel Lee, available June 2017 wherever
Harlequin® Special Edition books and ebooks are sold.

www.Harlequin.com

Celebrate 20 Years of

Love Inspired

Inspirational Romance to Warm Your Heart and Soul

Whether you love heart-pounding suspense, historically rich stories or contemporary heartfelt romances, Love Inspired® Books has it all!

Sign up for the Love Inspired newsletter at **www.Loveinspired.com** and connect with us to find your next great read from the **Love Inspired**, **Love Inspired Suspense** and **Love Inspired Historical** series.

 www.Facebook.com/LoveInspiredBooks

 www.Twitter.com/LoveInspiredBks

www.LoveInspired.com

LIBPA0517

THE WORLD IS BETTER WITH

Romance

Harlequin has everything from contemporary, passionate and heartwarming to suspenseful and inspirational stories.

Whatever your mood, we have a romance just for you!